MW01245498

Christmas Confessions

Astor Family Novel, Volume 1

J.M. Guilfoyle

Published by J.M. Guilfoyle, 2022.

This is a work of fiction. Similarities to real people, places, or events are entirely coincidental.

CHRISTMAS CONFESSIONS

First edition. October 21, 2022.

For my husband. My best friend and rock.

CHAPTER ONE
Where is the guest of honor?

Lucas

Lucas paced towards the Rielly Gallery's front windows in search of better cell reception.

"You're an idiot." Christian Astor, his best friend, assaulted him from behind.

Was Lucas an idiot? Yes. He didn't deny that. Granted, he had no basis for why he was one at this moment and didn't care. Gritting his teeth, Lucas checked his phone again. Five bars. Zero calls. Zero texts. Not even a direct message on any platforms. The damn thing had to be lying to him!

Wait. Of course!

Rielly Gallery was the centerpiece in an up-and-coming district in Brooklyn. A renovated warehouse, with an exterior of those highly sought after aged red brick and an interior filled with pillars and walls covered in new drywall all painted bright white. Blank canvases for whatever art was being featured that month. This month, the featured artist was a photojournalist who'd captured pictures from the last year in Syria.

Lucas remembered a time when the steel used to build warehouses caused havoc on cell phone signals, which could theoretically be the case. Steel was playing havoc on his cell phone signal.

Lack of cell reception was the only plausible reason Bella Astor, his other best friend and Christian's twin sister, was not chewing him the hell out.

No. Lucas thought of another reason.

Maybe that crafty blond socialite was torturing him. Making Lucas imagine all the ways she could eviscerate him for his role in bringing her to her mother's insane PR stunt.

He squinted at the cell phone screen, hoping to see the bars drop to zero, and was sorely disappointed, then asked, "Why am I an idiot?"

Chris fiddled with a wisp of light brown hair in the reflection of a sculpture. 'Sculpture' was a loose term for the metal monstrosity.

All the sun-bleached tones from summer finally faded from Christian's hair. Now fewer people mistook Lucas for Chris' twin. A thought Lucas never quite understood. Six inches separated the two boys in height, and where Chris had long, lean muscles, Lucas was broader, more muscular. Their most similar features were in their faces, but even then, they didn't look that similar.

"You're right. Let's see. Why are you an idiot today?" Chris moved to adjust the buttons on his tuxedo jacket and straightened his already perfectly situated vest. "How about this?"

Here it comes, Lucas thought.

"You should have just picked up my sister! Win-win. Bella gets here, more or less on time — "

Lucas added under his breath, "Would have helped more if the mayor was on time."

But Chris continued, uninhibited, "— and you would have had time, confined in your rusted out Corolla, to ask her the hell out!" He grabbed Lucas' tie and tightened it like a noose. "Bonus, the crap-olla might have broken down, and you would be forced to fend for your life with my crazy ass sister in arctic temperatures. Who knows *what* you would have had to resort to stay alive until the tow truck got there. And this entire fiasco might be over already. Because I would've accepted the award in Bella's place, there'd be *no* potential for my sister to screw everything up. And I would be free to take that brunette goddess home sooner rather than later."

"The server staring at you?" Lucas griped, ignoring the dig at his car. He loosened his tie.

"The one I'm about to get a drink from? Yes. That one." Chris flashed a wry smile, catching not only the girl in all black with a sleek brown ponytail but every other server in a ten-foot radius and a few of the Astor family friends as well. "Also, if you didn't catch it, I'm insinuating —"

Lucas slapped Chris' hand and backed away. A few heads turned in their direction. "I know what you're insinuating," Lucas hissed and stared at the ceiling. Heaven forbid Lucas would rather form an actual relationship with a woman than just have sex.

"What?" Chris asked. The sudden outburst caused more people to turn and watch them. "I've come to the conclusion you're the only guy that can tolerate Bella's specific brand of," Chris made a face Lucas couldn't put a name to, then gave up looking for the right words altogether.

Lucas checked his phone again. Still nothing. Not even an emoji. "How romantic. You want me to hook up with Bells because no one else can tolerate her."

"Hooking up with her might..."

"Don't finish that! You're a really wonderful brother." Lucas said sarcastically while simultaneously trying to keep his calm. "And so romantic."

"Says the man who is such a hopeless romantic he can't even ask the woman he loves out on a date. And he sees her daily."

When put like that, Lucas sounded like the biggest idiot in the world.

Chris steered him back towards the interior of the gallery. The brunette server mingling among the crowd disappeared from sight, so they stopped where a photo of Bella had hung until recently. Chris insisted the gallery move it and now they stared at a photo of a family huddled together.

The image of the earlier photo stayed burned into Lucas' mind.

Bella. Scrubs and a messy mass of light-colored hair covered in dark blood and crumpled against a stone wall. Rebar punctured the wall. Mere inches from losing Bells forever. Nightmares still plagued him.

"All I'm saying is you missed a golden opportunity with Bells. And this would have gone so much more smoothly if you had gone down and picked my dumbass sister up."

"I swear yesterday you said if I stepped foot at the screening event Bells' is hosting, I would, and I quote, 'never return because Bella is a succubus and I cannot say no to her.'"

"That is true, actually. You can't say no to Bells." Chris laughed at his own joke. They watched as the server he'd been eyeing all evening as they turned back into view. "Well, either way, I'd still be going home with miss...what do you think her name is?" Chris blew a ragged breath at the next enlarged, gritty gray-scale photo they passed. "You're whipped and not even dating Bells," Chris said dismally. "She smiles and bats those eyes at you, and you can barely muster a single word response. It's wretched. And I have had to watch it..." Chris stopped, making a point of counting ridiculously slowly on his fingers. "Twelve years."

These were all fair points. Lucas wasn't dating Bella. They had a dozen years of evidence that he couldn't say no to her. And he definitely turned to mush when she smiled at him.

For one very good reason. That smile, the real one with the dimples and laugh lines and the way her eyes sparkled, was nothing short of pure magic.

Lucas moved on to another photo down the wall, slowly making his way towards the small mass of people. Primarily the group was made up of board members of Astor Pharm and a few city council members.

"You should listen to me more often," Chris said. He continued following Lucas around the gallery.

"No, I shouldn't." Lucas scrutinized another portrait for signs of Bella's blond messy curls amid the rubble. He'd found her in two images. There was a third photograph somewhere in the exhibit where Bella delivered a baby in the back of a military humvee. Not the same socialite he'd met in college mere weeks after she'd been arrested for a fistfight in a nightclub. And that fight was only a whopping two days after crashing a

Porsche. Those few weeks defined her public image at the age of seventeen and carried through to this day.

Bella's name still brought the paparazzo out, looking for the next big celebrity scoop. This wasn't exactly an award garnering significant attention, so the few paparazzi milling around the fringes probably thought they could get some celeb gossip scoop.

"You never would have met Bells if it weren't for me," Christian chimed.

"We both still would have been in choir."

The continued silence from Bella agitated Lucas' unease more than Chris' anxiety-fueled yammering.

Lucas and Chris kept on the edges. There were clusters of VIPs and a smattering of reporters he recognized, mostly associated with newspapers.

"You're right," Chris said. "You would have met Bells in choir and without me and been utterly defenseless. No buffer against those deranged Astor genes."

Together they turned a corner, and Chris appeared to give up on Lucas. He flipped a switch and turned his oozing charm on the brunette server as she passed in front of them with a tray of full champagne glasses. She winked at Chris and he snagged a new flute.

"You need to worry less. Have a drink." He tried to shove a flute in Lucas' hand.

With a shake of his head, Lucas set it back on the tray.

"Come on," Chris whined.

"No, thank you. I prefer being sober," Lucas said and immediately realized how stupid that probably sounded. This was potentially the best time to have a drink. Dull the edge of what's to come. Because something was coming. He felt it.

"This is supposed to be a celebration."

"Sure," Lucas said, noticing that Chris had yet to finish charming the lovely brunette server. A sure sign of how preoccupied Christian Astor indeed was. "And you're not worried?"

"No." Chris waved off the comment.

Lucas finally could spot when his friend was lying, so he asked, "Do you remember Etiquette School?"

Chris choked on the question and champagne, every ounce of coolness gone. The server excused herself quietly, giggling as she moved on to another group.

"Yes. I remember. No one can forget Etiquette School," Chris replied, still trying to clear his throat. "This is nothing like Etiquette School."

Lucas wasn't so sure. "Both were planned by your mother." Somehow, the former had been backed by the entire family, including Bella's father. "In both, we knew exactly how Bella felt beforehand." Pissed off.

Chris interrupted, "She's getting a freaking award tonight. There is no reason for her to be pissed about getting an award!"

Finally, after all the stressing out over this ceremony, Lucas let out a slightly deranged laugh. And it grew the more flustered Chris got.

"Stop. Okay, this is completely different." Chris said and grimaced into his flute.

There it was. The light bulb moment. Chris figured it out. Yes, Bella was receiving an award for humanitarian services to the city, but this wasn't all that different from Etiquette School. Someone forcing Bella's hand never ended well for anyone.

How Lucas let himself get roped into this was beyond him.

Lucas sighed. He got one last nervous laugh and said, "We're so screwed."

"Not the screwed I was hoping for." Chris gulped the rest of his champagne.

Lucas sighed. "Didn't need to hear that."

Chris broke away, his hand held out at the mass of people heading towards the pair. "Mayor Hulme! What an honor it is to see you again!"

A sheen of sweat coated Lucas' hands. The mayor arrived in a blaze of assistants, guards, and a plain black and white suit to complement his slicked back light brown hair and reemerging tan from his vacation in the tropics.

And they were still down one guest of honor.

Mayor Hulme charmed Christian with witty repartee while Lucas stood on the sidelines, ignored by all the mayor's assistants and photographers, until a whispered, "Mr. Holt?" caught his attention. Daniel emerged from the shadows around the portrait Lucas had been staring at, startling Lucas. Though not technically the Astor family's assistant any longer, Daniel still did many things for Christian he'd done all the twins' lives.

Lucas and Chris turned, Chris excusing himself from the mayor.

Kind, dark eyes carried a hint of uncertainty as Daniel smoothed his black hair down in a single swipe.

"Daniel?" The man was noticeably alone. "Where's Bella?" Lucas' heart stopped. "Please tell me you didn't come back without Bella." The man practically raised the twins. He attended more of the twins' recitals and competitions than their father. How could he, of all people, not convince Bella to attend and accept one little plaque? He was Bella's secondary father figure! And the key to their entire plan to get Bella here without incident so they could placate Lina.

"Did you lose my sister?" Chris whispered. Behind them, the mayor's assistants snapped pictures on their phones. Lucas imagined the hashtags and commentary flying off into the web. Daniel looked at his feet while Chris continued, "Because there is no way anyone can just lose my sister. She is far too obnoxious to not be seen and heard."

"You're not helping," Lucas ground his teeth.

"I delivered Miss Astor here. That was the deal." Daniel smirked, his eyes sliding to where Mrs. Lina Astor gabbed with her board members of one of her charitable foundations. She had a knack for also maintaining a hawk-eye on the trio of men while she talked.

"Is it getting hot in here?" Lucas mumbled, trying to break away from Lina Astor's demonic stare. "Wait. No."

"You, Mr. Holt, can convince Miss Astor to make her appearance. Or shall I ask Mrs. Astor to fetch Miss Bella?"

Lucas' stomach dropped out from under him. He should have grabbed a champagne flute before. Stress tore his stomach apart, and this single night might just give him an ulcer.

"No!" Lucas turned, looking for any signs of Bella. Whispers from behind him let him know he'd made yet another mistake. "No." He repeated more quietly. "I got it."

Daniel nodded towards where a passing blond server carrying a tray of champagne flutes had come. The kitchen door flapping behind the server.

"Ah, mother." Casually sipping from his flute, Chris added his own grin at Lucas.

Best friend indeed.

Lucas turned to Daniel. "You distract Mrs. Astor. I'll get Bella without making a scene."

"Thank you, Mr. Holt."

A mischievous glint in Daniel's eyes made Lucas regret not going down to the clinic. Getting roped into staying there was suddenly the much better option.

CHAPTER TWO
Anyone order a side of spectacle?

Bella

Bella wondered whose brilliant idea it was to host an award ceremony at a photography exhibition about a war at a modern art gallery. She never — not in a million years — would have gotten in the car with Daniel if she had known *what* exhibit was showing. The exhibit information was conveniently missing anytime anyone (Chris, her mother, Daniel) brought up the award ceremony.

A part of Bella knew she shouldn't have trusted Daniel. It was probably her mother's idea to use that sweet man to twist her arm and emotions into showing up when she'd already said, 'Hell no! Chris could accept that dumbass award' when her mother brought it up at tea.

Mental note: In the future, decline all new 'traditions' with her mother. Never once had her mother wanted to have 'tea' until two weeks ago. Bella should have known her mother's invitation was nothing more than a plot.

Bella caught sight of her mother and the board for the Frazier Foundation (one of her mother's charitable foundations) in a corner, completely ignoring the entire Syria exhibit.

Beside her, Daniel searched for her brother, so Bella took advantage of the distraction and bolted for the kitchens, mixed herself a quick drink, and plopped on the counter. Bella would hide and check in with her partner, Alicia until someone needed her for the literal handing over of an award, handshake, and stupid photo op. Of course, Alicia was busy or didn't hear her phone. Bella left a voicemail.

Bored and waiting for a callback, Bella sat on the icy stainless steel counters in the kitchen and swiped her long trench coat back and forth, singing off pitch. Long dark blond curls tied down in low pigtails were now falling apart from latent steam as the serving staff uncovered hor d'oeuvres in the kitchen.

The door flew open to reveal Lucas. He stood there, tapping his foot and scowling at her. And he looked *good*. His suit was crisp and fresh-looking even after a day of meetings and tailing after her brother. He'd even forgotten to remove the obnoxiously red candy cane tie she gave him. The one he'd balked at on the first night of their Twelve Movies of Christmas tradition, and yet here he was wearing it.

Bella: 1000 points

Lucas: Uh. Actually, she didn't know. They were probably even. Bella kept every single gift Lucas had given her and wore even the most ostentatious clothes he'd given her without remorse.

Bella raised her glass to him and sang, "Fa la la la la la la la...la?" Then wiggled her ass on the freezing counter a little extra at the end for effect. It worked.

His scowl deepened. But his baby blue eyes were trying very hard not to laugh, which made Bella more determined to break him. He would laugh, or she would eat that fuzzy Santa hat she left in Daniel's car.

Lucas pointed out the door. "The party is out there."

"Last time I checked, I was the party." Bella tipped her glass again. Her phone rang, volume turned up to max, but she pushed the call to voicemail. Then gave Lucas a sultry eyebrow waggle. "Going to come party with me, Midwest?"

"Your mother will boil both of us alive if you don't come out now and accept this award." Sure enough, Lucas checked over his shoulder. Mother dearest must be on the warpath. "The mayor is here!" he said.

Bella took a moment as if she was considering Lucas' words, but really she was busy evaluating Lucas. He looked freaking phenomenal in the silverish gray three-piece suit, including her awesome tie. Lucas should have girls falling at his feet with his deep voice, golden hair, and clear blue eyes. One might call him dreamy if he weren't her best friend and currently trying to drag her out for torture.

Glass already half empty, Bella took a big swig. "Nah. Mother doesn't cook. She might freeze us or feed us to wolves or..." His arms tightened around his chest. Bella grumbled, "No silent night for me."

And then he did it again. Aww. Fidgety Lucas meant a very stressed out Lucas. "Gosh, you're hard to please. Not even a smile because I'm here and haven't made a huge scene? I mean, who sends a director to wrangle up a lowly little doctor like me?"

Bella topped off her drink from a tumbler with ice sitting next to her.

The joke didn't work. Lucas silently glared back at Bella, his lips pressed into a tight line. Eventually, he leaned into the frame, holding her gaze until Bella broke and glanced down into the vibrant drink in her hand.

"That isn't one of the dresses your mother sent over, is it?" Lucas said and nodded at the flap of her trench coat left open. Bright green and red had been peeking through.

She whipped the coat closed. No, it definitely wasn't a dress from her mother. "You don't work for my mother, Mr. Holt, Director of Distribution and Sales. And my wardrobe is not part of your duties."

"Do you want your mother to come back here? She really will..."

Bella sharply inhaled, preparing to scream and beckon her mother. Lucas launched himself into the kitchen and clamped her mouth shut. "Please. Don't."

Bella won. She couldn't care less if her mother came in. Whenever they got around to giving her the dumbass plaque, everyone would be pissed at her, anyway. If she didn't embarrass the hell out of her family, her dress would do the job just fine.

"Chris was right," Lucas whispered in her ear.

A shiver ran down her spine, but Bella suppressed it and pried his hand from her mouth to ask, "What was he right about?"

"You're pure evil."

"He didn't say that," Bella said and fixed his lopsided tie. He'd been fidgeting and trying to fix it himself without a mirror, or Chris had 'fixed' the tie and tried to strangle Lucas instead.

"He implied it."

Bella couldn't argue. For her brother, she always was especially devious.

"What are you doing back here?" Lucas pleaded.

Wait staff carrying trays of empty champagne flutes ducked around Lucas, swapping their trays for trays of hor d'oeuvres. As one server passed by, Bella grabbed a piece of mini toast with lobster, popped it in her mouth, and with her mouth full, said, "Snatching up the freshest food before the masses have a...what?"

Impatience boiled over in Lucas. He cocked his head, and she'd attack him if she had access to a pillow. Maybe she could drag him to the gym instead of slinking out to accept a dumb medal or whatever. They could wrestle it out for real.

Tonight, though, she had a sinking feeling she wouldn't win if she started a fight, pillow or not.

Bella shook her phone at him. "I had to make a call. *I'm* not even supposed to be here. *I'm* supposed to be doing the holiday health screening event. The doctor Christian placed there is a..." Lucas rolled his eyes again.

"Don't give me that look!" Bella whined. "That doctor can't even explain why a blood draw is necessary to one of the community members! Mr. Keeler was screaming at everyone that they were trying to steal his blood."

Lucas almost broke.

"I should be *there*. Not *here!* Can't you just whisk me away back to the health screening event and after I promise to split a pizza and six-pack with you?"

Any sane person would think begging was below her station in life, but no one wanted Bella at this awards ceremony. Least of all, Bella. Plus, Christian and Lucas didn't want to be stuck here making sure she didn't do something considered 'embarrassing' or 'over theatrical' or 'dramatic.' The nicest terms people had for categorizing Bella's actions.

It would be easier and less problematic if she weren't at the ceremony. No one said *she* had to accept said plaque. Christian could very well have accepted on her behalf.

Of course, pizza and beer were not a hugely attractive offer, but he knew it was the best she could do after swearing off using her trust fund money. Right now, her only other option was to attempt to win over Lucas with her charming personality. Judging by the death stare boring straight into Bella's soul, her offer was out of the question.

Bella cursed Daniel's emotional manipulation again.

"I can't do that," Lucas said. "Your mother..."

"Ugh! You don't work for my mother." Bella moaned and kicked her legs.

"How adult of you," he said, pointing at her flailing legs like she was a child trapped in a thirty year old's body. "And I don't work for you either." His eyes narrowed on her, though he did smile. At least she finally broke him.

"Come on, Lucas! I can't go out there. Have some mercy. It's the holidays!"

Lucas held out his hand for her. Then he replied, "You just need to step out this door and accept the plaque from the mayor, Bells. That's it."

He broke out the nickname. Low blow.

Begrudgingly, Bella took his hand. "Then you'll drive me back? You! Not Daniel. Not a taxi."

"Then I'll drive you back to the rec center. You can explain phlebotomy and blood analysis and vaccinate people to your heart's content. I'll even treat you to pizza and your favorite hard cider."

"Fancy." Bella threw an elbow into his side and gave him a lopsided smirk.

She clutched at the drink in her hand, and Lucas responded by squeezing her other arm, then looping it around his arm. At the door, Bella stood on her tiptoes, peering through the window at the life she had left behind. The life she didn't belong to anymore and avoided at all costs.

A room full of socialites. People who cared about nothing more than exterior beauty, social standing, and net worth. Dresses that cost more than cars. Judgment. Gossip. Everything portrayed in the media was only the tip of the iceberg for the privileged class.

"Can I place any and all blame on you for anything I do once I step outside those doors?" She asked. Bella took a gulp of the bright red, tart cherry drink.

Lucas grinned his most charming grin. Damn him. Two in one conversation. He was finally warming up. Thank God he could never begrudge her for long. "Congratulations, Dr. Astor." Then he tugged on her jacket's shoulder. "You *are* wearing a dress, right?"

"Sure."

A whole two steps into the gallery, and they were assaulted by a nearly life-size photo of Bella, which she hadn't noticed earlier in her haste to find a hiding spot.

At first glance, the photo in front showed a pile of rubble and billowing dust overhead. Bella's eyes took a moment to adjust, and she realized not all the debris was brick and rock.

There were people. Pieces and whole. The dust settled on bodies thrown into walls and rubble indiscriminately.

Six months ago seemed like a lifetime ago until she was face to face with herself in stark black and white. Black streaked her head and hair. Slumped against a torn apart wall. Syria. Outside the health center.

A rush of emotion left Bella limp.

Lucas tried to keep her moving when he realized why she'd stopped. His eyes followed hers. "This...you weren't supposed to—"

"It's fine." Bella put on a brave face and tried to brush off the remnants of her time overseas before it threatened to engulf her. Her time in Frontier Doctors became a time her family ignored. Gone nearly five years was treated almost like it didn't happen.

"Come on. You don't have to—Bells, I'm so sorry. Chris had them move the photos with you to the back because he assumed you'd stay in the front..."

She ended his nervous rambling by pecking him on the cheek.

"Lucas, it's fine. I'm fine. It's all fine."

"Yes, you sound fine." He straightened his suit coat nervously, constantly tugging and pulling on it when his nerves took over. "I'll go get Christian. Or do you want..."

She shook her head, and the curls of her pigtails tickled her neck. Lucas understood. He always understood. He could leave Bella to her thoughts to search for her brother. She'd prefer the quiet than the crowd and spotlight until the last minute and would stay right there, as promised, trying to reconcile her two lives, past and present, until someone told her they were ready for her.

That day in the picture was a blur. Hell, the days all blurred together around that time. The days in the hospital, the surgery, the flights home. Syria seemed like a strange dream that didn't happen until her shoulder hurt. Pain twinged her shoulder now.

Her thoughts returned to the day, struggling to remember what had happened. She'd been on the edge of their allocated zone, but the blast was too close. Enough to knock her over and send debris flying all around her.

Seeing herself lying against the remnants of a building was surreal.

Someone cleared their throat behind her and brought Bella back to reality.

"When I came for the opening, you were up front, where you belong."

Bella wheeled around. Her hand trembled at that voice. She clutched harder to the glass, praying she'd heard wrong.

"Bells?"

No, she hadn't heard wrong!

Bella turned and found Preston Warren and his ridiculously perfect deep dark hair, combed back with the perfect amount of stubble along his chiseled jawline, making him look chic instead of sloppy. Eyes so dark they almost looked black, blending perfectly with his hair staring at her. Pres was still as perfect as freaking ever. "Wow. You look..."

Five years' worth of repressed rage grabbed at Bella's and set the world spinning.

CHAPTER THREE
Ditched again

Bella

Five years earlier
(Or really, Four years, 11 months, and ten days earlier. But who's counting?)

Bella sighed and fixated on the dozen Christmas trees lining the Astor mansion ballroom walls every few feet. Pretty, glittery LED lit trees, crisscrossed with gold ribbon and an ungodly amount of golden glass balls, sat against a backdrop of dark cherry wood paneling and the parquet floor. Her mother's predictable, lifeless Christmas decorations.

In any typical year, the Astor Holiday Gala would have started the season of holiday galas in the greater New York area. By the second week of December, Lina could be rid of any trace of the wretchedly cheerful holiday.

With Bella heading off for her first tour with Frontier Doctors, her father insisted on pushing back the gala to the last possible second. The day before Christmas Eve. One party, dual purposes. More holiday cheer than Lina could stand in the mansion. Maybe the only good thing about this gala coming so late in the month.

The hem of her dress and petticoat brushed against her thighs. Bella would never admit that she liked the black halter dress her mother sent over. The lace top actually complimented her nicely.

"So?" Lucas asked, dropping a flourished metal rental chair behind Bella, then pulled up a second one for himself. "Did you find your..." He caught himself on his words. He couldn't finish that statement with something nice, like 'better half,' about Preston Warren. Not without gagging.

Bella smiled and saved him by saying, "MIA."

Her feet throbbed insolently. She tried to ease gracefully into the chair but ended up falling instead. After another loop around the party searching for her wayward Preston, the backs of those obscenely uncomfortable Ralph and Russo's gouged into the back of her heels.

The Astor Mansion had hundreds of hiding places where people could congregate away from prying eyes. Bella was fed up looking. She searched the dining room, library, study, and kitchen. In those few rooms, she'd stepped into a lot of things going on, and none of it involved her boyfriend.

Bella flicked off the back of one shoe; blisters and sores tore open as she let the shoe drop.

Trading her shoe for the glass of dark liquor in Lucas' hand, Lucas bent, gently removing the other.

"You leave tomorrow," he commented.

The remark stung.

Yes, she left tomorrow, and her boyfriend was missing. He'd ditched her, and for what? A new client? Existing client? Something else?

Or did he go running when Lucas brought Bella her first drink of the night? Could Pres, as her boyfriend, really not stand Lucas that much?

All the man did was bring her a glass of her favorite bourbon. Or had it solely been Lucas' presence?

Apparently, Preston couldn't be cordial to Lucas for a single night. Not even for her.

Preston was her first best friend; since they were five years old. Lucas only picked up that title of best friend when Preston became too busy chasing other girls to be bothered with Bella. It would be nice if Pres remembered that.

"These blisters will be hell when you're on your feet all day." Lucas' thumb grazed the side of an intact blister, bringing Bella back from her thoughts.

She winced and took a large gulp of bourbon. "Yes, I am sure my mother cared so much about the wellbeing of my feet when she picked this crap out." Bella emptied the glass, shaking it at him. Lucas glanced at the glass and shook his head. "Come on," Bella whined, but Lucas shook his head at her again. "We both know that you, Mr. Holt, know how to treat a girl." Bella whipped out a dazzling smile, praying genetics granted her half the power her brother held in his smile. The man had to know she needed more alcohol to get through the rest of this party.

Instead, Lucas gave her a hard pinch on her toe, grabbing both feet and resting them on his lap, then asked, "Going to send out a search party?"

Damn. If Bella wanted more bourbon, she'd have to get up off her lazy butt to get it herself.

"Not at this late stage in the game."

What *was* the point now? Guests were starting their gracious exits to Lina Astor. Her father, Eli, and Chris were both as noticeably absent as Preston.

Deep strokes traveled along her foot. Lucas hesitated at the top of her foot and said, "I heard a rumor you need a ride to the airport."

Goosebumps broke out along her arms as his thumb traveled back down. The feeling faded as soon as he stopped at the bottom, waiting for her answer.

Whether from the alcohol or sheer disappointment, Bella's eyes glazed over. She stared into the empty tumbler forlornly and took a deep breath. "Pres is working tomorrow."

"Preston," Lucas dropped her foot to ask, "is working? On Christmas Eve? Instead of taking his girlfriend to the airport?"

After a deep sigh, Bella said, "I don't know. Some big case? It's not for Astor Pharm?" The recently appointed 'Manager of National Distribution,' Lucas J. Holt, might have heard something in a meeting, and it just had slipped his mind until she asked.

But he shook his head.

The thought crossed her mind again that Preston had planned something huge for her departure. A kind of last-minute proposal at the gate. Everyone, and she meant everyone, expected the spectacle tonight at the party. And that was the only reason she'd worn heels and picked a dress from the wardrobe her mother sent, spent an obscene amount of time on her hair and makeup. All for Lucas, apparently.

Bella fiddled with her empty ring finger again.

Honestly, she didn't even know if she wanted to marry Preston. As a descendant of the historic Beaumont family, she was supposed to marry a guy like Preston Warren. Be an upstanding wife and not make waves. Bella Astor was supposed to be the complete opposite of who she really was. On paper, Preston Warren was the perfect husband for her...family.

If her grandfather were still with the world, he'd never have let her enlist with Frontier Doctors. Hell, she might not have finished her medical degree.

A thought struck Bella. "Let's go get tacos! Let's go to Otto's! I'll pay this time!"

"We went there for lunch!" Lucas laughed.

"Come on! When's the next time I'm going to get tacos?"

Frontier Doctors wasn't sending her anywhere where tacos were easily accessible.

"Plus," Bella said, giving him her best pout, "I need to apologize somehow for missing Christmas."

"That I cannot fault you for. Missing the Holt Christmas Extravaganza to go...wherever the heck you're going and help people is a worthy cause."

Last year was the closest she'd come to missing the Holt Family Christmas since meeting Lucas. Every year, the twins borrowed their father's jet to take Lucas home to Kalamazoo, and every year he invited them to stay and celebrate. To have real family time during the holidays. Something the twins hadn't gotten since they were five, maybe six, years old.

And for some unfathomable reason, last year she'd agreed to go with Preston to the Warren's family charity ball on Christmas Eve instead of going home with Lucas. Chris stayed behind in New York with Bella because...well, there'd been some flimsy reason.

However, Pres spent most of the time meeting new donors and benefactors and constantly pushing Bella aside.

After hours at the Warren Ball by herself, Chris whispered, "Dad's jet is fueled up."

"Where would we…?"

Chris planted his phone, screen lit with a picture of the twins flanking Lucas at the end of her nose. All three were bundled in layers of thermals and topped with waterproof coats and colorful beanies. Together, they held up a two-foot bass between the three of them.

"I have a desire to go fishing," her brother said, then jiggled her.

That was funny, Bella thought. Chris rarely had a desire to go fishing. Ever.

"*Ice* fishing."

As if she didn't understand.

No, she got it. They were in danger of missing their yearly ice fishing trip with Lucas.

"I promised Pres."

Why had she stayed at the Astor Gala for so long?

Honestly, she'd rather sit in a little tent with instant coffee, freezing her ass off with Lucas and Chris. Hours' worth of trading watch on their rods was far more appealing than the damn charity event for another second.

"And," Chris added, "Pres ditched you." Her brother had been utterly gleeful about ditching the Warren Ball as well as he pried the glass from her hand.

When Pres had found out she'd left the gala, he was so pissed she'd ditched him to fly to the middle of nowhere. But he'd ditched her back then, and he ditched her again tonight!

"Tacos and churros!" Bella exclaimed as she bounced on her seat, scooting as close as she could to Lucas, pleading with her eyes and a toothy grin. "Please. Please, please, please! Churros. Churros!"

"Okay." Lucas laughed and tried to stop the bouncing, which was drawing more attention to them than he found comfortable. Lowering his voice, Lucas said, "I will agree to tacos and churros if you make one more pass to look for Warren. Man's going to give me hell for taking his girlfriend either way. You can tell him I didn't steal you." He poked her cheek playfully. "I'll go tell Chris and Eli we're leaving."

Bella was out of the chair, shoes in hand, and practically running through the thinning crowd of guests when Lucas caught her hand again. "One more thing. You, Miss Astor," Lucas brushed her nose, "have to watch one more movie with me before you leave. And I get to pick a movie."

"Movie?"

The evening was turning around! They wouldn't finish their yearly movie marathon, but at least she'd have one more bright spot before leaving the country.

Lucas kept going, "You're going to sleep on the plane anyway, and Chris cleared our schedules tomorrow." That meant Lucas's flight home wasn't until the afternoon since Chris hated being up before 11 am on a non-work day (of course, he made an exception for seeing Bella off).

Then Lucas continued, "I think Chris had another surprise for you tonight. Ah. One more thing." Lucas scooped up the shoes from her hand. "I'm confiscating these."

Thank god, no more foot torture. She'd rather brave snow-crusted sidewalks barefoot than wear those shoes again. Lucas might piggyback her out to his car if she was lucky.

"Deal!" She pecked him on the forehead. "Ooooh, you're the best!"

Bella ruffled Lucas' hair and hopped around the ballroom like a kid searching for their friends in a hide-and-seek game. Alas, Bella combed more rooms and found no sign of her missing boyfriend. Preston wouldn't have left, but there were many places he could be. Taking a call, working in a different study or even a bedroom. Preston knew the Astor mansion better than Bella at this point. There were entire wings she could go searching in, but she did *not* have the patience for that right now.

And she didn't exactly care anymore, either. If Pres couldn't be bothered to spend Bella's last night in the states with her, she was determined to have fun.

Bella took the stairs two at a time.

Her mother's Christmas decorations only crept up as far as the landing on the second floor. Lighted garland twined around the handrail and abruptly stopped at the top. The plush runner in the second-floor hallway, a deep burgundy, made Bella's steps silent.

Her childhood bedroom was just up the hall, closest to the staircase. A hand-painted polka dot B from her door sat discarded on the floor in front of her room. Where the letter hung, a faint shadow was left behind. Bella picked it up and replaced the B on the door.

Bella paused at the door to listen for any noises over the party below but heard nothing.

She kept an eye on the hallway in the event any partygoers were sneaking around. When she thought the coast was clear, Bella opened the door to her room and backed in. Not bothering to turn on the light, Bella crept through the darkness. Her coat lay across the chair to her desk, past her rumpled duvet and pillows.

Really? Someone used her childhood room? They couldn't have used Chris'? Less pink frills and ballet awards and more stench of his past exploits.

Whoever it was, they were passed out amidst an overpowering smell of alcohol. Bella finished crossing her modestly sized room (considering her parents owned a mansion), grabbed her coat, and froze. The guy groaned and turned over. A mess of dark hair stuck up. "Bells?" He moaned and shook the woman next to him.

Bella flipped the switch on her desk lamp. The harsh, tiny light flared almost as much as Bella.

"You asshole!" Bella screeched and considered ripping the desk lamp from the wall socket to throw at him. "You...you fucking asshole!" She grabbed frames from her bookshelf. "You promised me!" Each word was punctuated with a new frame careening across the room, ending in a spray of glass. "No! Cheating! You'd! Changed! Really?"

"Bella?" Preston flailed for cover. During a reprieve, while Bella took her coat, pulling angrily at a seam, Pres rolled out of bed, naked, which set Bella off again. Books careened across the room this time since she'd run out of frames.

They landed with a thunk and dented the wall. One bounced and broke a reading lamp.

The woman in the bed screamed.

"Bella?" Preston said and almost sounded confused.

Bella's duvet came hurling at her as the naked woman hopped out of Bella's bed and yelped, "You psycho!"

Holy shit. That black hair and tan and tone? Bella's vision went red.

Vaguely, she heard people crashing up the stairs.

"Trish? You want to see psycho?" Bella had an entire shelf of books. She could show the woman psycho.

Arms grabbed Bella from behind, trapping her.

"You couldn't wait for me to leave, could you?" Bella said. Then tried to pry whoever was holding her tight.

"Bella? I... You..." Preston's words were drowned out by Bella again. "I thought..." Preston's haze didn't help his cause.

"Trish?" Chris said. And his voice was the only one Bella heard clearly.

The only voice that stopped her heart hammering in her chest.

"I can explain." Preston rushed to put on his boxers and pants. "Bella, seriously. I thought it was y—"

"I should let Bells go," Lucas grunted, trying to keep Bella from pouncing.

When Bella broke down, and the fight drained out of her, Lucas pulled her to standing and drew her close.

Bella stifled sobs and clenched and unclenched fistfuls of Lucas' suit jacket.

"Bells." Preston's use of her nickname broke her.

Bella reached around Lucas to the bookshelf behind Lucas, grabbed another small paperback, and twisted in Lucas' arms. "And of all people, you slept with Trish?"

Chris said, "Give me the ring." His ordinarily cool voice was downright arctic. "Trish, give me the ring."

"Christian. I can explain too." Trisha quickly pulled on her slinky, sparkly silver dress.

"There's not a single explanation I'll believe." Chris held his hand out.

What? Did she mistake Pres for Chris? Pres was five inches taller, dark-haired, and had that stupid stubble he loved. Like the complete opposite of Chris. Chris was clean-shaven and dark blond. There was no world in which *they* could be mistaken for each other, no matter how drunk Trisha was.

Trish begged, "What? No! Christian, please."

Present Day

The weight of that night almost five years ago hit Bella like a train. Raw anger twisted into hate that stayed coiled in her chest. Preston fucking Warren stood next to her and was — what? — trying to charm her? Five years too late for that.

The man that age eight promised he'd never hurt her. Age ten insisted they would get married one day. At sixteen, beat the ever-loving shit out of the first guy to ask her out because of some crazy rumor that started at their boarding school. At age twenty-two, he vowed not to sleep with another girl because he realized how much he loved Bella. And he didn't, as far as she knew. Six months later, Preston asked her out at her twenty-third birthday party.

And at age twenty-five, Pres slept with her brother's fiancé. The rest of that night was an alcohol fueled rage that Lucas later pieced together for Bella on the phone after her first few weeks in Frontier Doctors.

Now, her nails dug into the glass, slipping along the smooth surface. Her own blood-soaked body slumped in the picture in her peripheral vision. Pres, about to say something else incredibly witty or charming, stopped short as the bright red liquid launched into his perfect, pompous, pretty playboy face. Red dye stained the entire front of his suit. An eerie, stunned silence took over the gallery.

Then shards of glass bounced from the floor at Preston's feet.

CHAPTER FOUR
Thirty seconds of perfection

Lucas

Judging by Lina Astor's almost genuine delight, Mayor Hulme was in the throes of a fantastic story. Chris stayed off to the side, his attention split between his mother and Lucas approaching.

"We're all set." Lucas clapped his hands together. "Bella's out of the kitchen and —"

Glass shattered on the cement floor. Turning meant seeing; seeing meant knowing what happened. If he didn't turn around, he never had to know what happened.

"Thirty seconds," Lucas swore under his breath.

"Since you left Bells' side? More like ten." Chris dropped his flute into Daniel's hand and strode to his sister.

Lucas, trailing only by a pace or two, said, "Remember when you said this would go fine?"

"I said no such thing," Chris corrected.

"No, this afternoon at the office. You said this would go fine. No problems whatsoever."

Flashes were going off from paparazzi and cell phones. People were murmuring. Fortunately, pillars and art pieces blocked many guests' view. But either way, this was not good. No matter

35

what Daniel did to help stave off reporters or paparazzi, Bella's actions were going up everywhere at the speed of tweeting, texting, and other social media posts.

Daniel pulled out his phone to call security. Astor private security and, undoubtedly, any security within the art gallery.

"I was also complaining about how bat shit crazy my attempted womb usurper was. I believe I even called her murderous."

Well, if Lucas ever doubted it before, he didn't now. "She looks murderous."

They couldn't cross the gallery quick enough.

"Have you not learned anything? You can't take your eyes off Bella."

"Excuse me?" Lucas fought the urge to tackle Christian and said, "She's been an adult the entire..."

That didn't sound right.

"What I meant to say was..."

Lucas realized he was out of luck with ways to defend himself. Fine. He had a sibling, too, and knew how these arguments went. "You know what?" And as soon as they stopped next to Bella, Lucas wheeled on Chris. "You had the curator move the picture to the back of the exhibit."

Place the blame elsewhere. Classic sibling technique.

"You're blaming me for this?" Chris squealed and grabbed Bella by the shoulders.

Lucas snapped one hand to Bella's waist. "Yeah, I am."

Bella rifled through her pockets, probably looking for anything to throw. Cell phones were a good weight and enough to hurt. Since meeting Bella, he'd witnessed her throw and break her fair share of phones. Keys worked well too. She'd even taken off and thrown her shoes at people, so he caught her wrist, sliding his fingers over her warm skin, and held her still. She clawed at his suit jacket for freedom.

"Warren, always a pleasure." Lucas turned Bells away before she acted on any more impulses and led her away from Warren and towards the unforgiving crowd taking pictures.

Lina tore through the gathering crowds. Renewed flashes lit Bella's face.

Chris buzzed around his sister, primping her hair. Daniel joined them, blocking the photographers as best he could while he and Lucas ambushed her.

"Hands off!" She smacked them all away from her jacket and hair.

"Bells. One photo. One little teeny tiny little photo op, where we're not throwing things." Chris used that same dazzling smile he wowed the board of directors with whenever they brought up a topic he hated. The same one he'd perfected on the women he took to bed. It worked on almost everyone except Bella. At most, it distracted his twin through pure annoyance.

When Bella turned on Chris, Lucas ripped apart the tie of her coat around her waist. Daniel tore the trench coat down Bella's arms.

And they all froze because Bella...was an elf. She was missing her hat and ears, but she was definitely, undeniably dressed as an elf. Bright green dress trimmed in red with a white furry collar, faux buttons, and a black belt cinching her waist. The only forgivable item she wore was low hunter green heels.

This was literally a new level of hell.

Mere feet away, Lina gasped in unadulterated horror at her oldest child. "Oh, dear Lord. Is this some new form of punishment?"

Absolutely hands down, the best way to attract what little attention from the crowd they didn't already have. And *Bella's* mother constantly complained that someone needed to do 'damage control' on Bella when Lina couldn't maintain her own composure?

"Merry Christmas, Mother," Bella said.

Then, of all the many things Bella could have done, she fucking curtsied.

This, right here, would give him the ulcer.

Lina Astor was at a loss for words.

Chris smacked his lips and said, "Mother sent dresses."

"I told you I was working," Bella shrugged calmly. Calmly! Like this was nothing.

"You agreed," the panic raised Chris' voice almost an entire octave higher than normal.

"I did no such thing."

That was true. Bella had refused all the original invitations, and no one knew what Daniel said to get her in the car.

"Bells," Christian seemed to debate the pros and cons of trying to cover the costume. Though what was the point when everyone in the gallery had seen her now? "Just one photo. No vulgarity..."

"Are you suggesting I don't know how to conduct myself in polite society?" Bella feigned shock, then weighed every next word carefully against Chris. "It's as if I wasn't forced into Etiquette School."

No one said a word. The mask, Bella's pissed off, and publicly famous scowl crossed her face.

Daniel broke the strained silence with, "Did you just throw wine on Mr. Warren."

"It was not wine. It was a cranberry spritzer." She fluffed her brilliantly blonde curls. "As if I'd drink when I'm *planning* to return to *work*!"

"Miss Astor!" Mayor Hulme said as he broke into their semicircle, oblivious to their drama. "How festive!" He grabbed Bella's hand with vigor.

Bella flipped a switch. The bitter smile was gone, replaced with Astor charm. "Mayor Hulme. You know, we should make this quick. The children at Levvy Rec Center were super disappointed this little elf..." — oh my god, she curtsied again but cutely — "...had to run all the way here."

"My." Hulme maintained his composure, even beaming at her. "We should have done this at the Rec Center! I haven't been there since the ribbon cutting ceremony!"

Another server, not the woman Chris worked his charm on earlier, passed with new flutes. Chris stopped the woman with a touch of the elbow, took a flute, and downed the contents in three gulps before returning the empty flute to her tray.

"I'm CEO, and yet my sister will be the end of my career. Not because of an arrest or fight. Because of an elf costume."

Lucas grabbed his own flute and said, "Could be worse."

"How?"

"The dress covers her..." Lucas gestured towards Bella's lower half. "And she didn't murder the mayor for not calling her Dr. Astor." A miracle in and of itself.

"I'm not sure that helps." Chris' gaze flicked to his mother, and Lucas followed. Lina was already in the midst of damage control.

CHAPTER FIVE

Aftermath (Probably should have slept in instead)

Bella

Bella jolted. The alarm on her phone blared. It was 6:40 AM. Shit! That was her last alarm for her morning sequence. She's somehow slept through them all! She was going to be late. Popping off her bed, Bella raced around her apartment, toothbrush in her mouth, elf dress still on. Bella searched for any scraps of caffeine or sustenance in empty cabinets. Nothing. In the most literal sense. She seriously needed to go grocery shopping.

Sunlight filtered through condensation ladened windows. Even with all the bright morning light, Bella almost tripped over her unopened Christmas Decorations boxes stacked in the corner of her kitchen. Her entire apartment was long and narrow, making every piece of furniture easy to trip over. Her couch or an end table took her out more than she'd care to admit in a sleep deprived state.

Last night had been a rare night Lucas didn't spend the night on her couch. She remembered returning to the health screening event with him only to find the event closed, and then there was beer, and then...nothing. A haze dropped over the entire night as if it were a dream. There was a vague sense of something utterly terrible happening.

Bella pathetically threw the dress across her bedroom, missing her hamper, grabbed a fresh pair of scrubs from her dresser, and threw her hair up in a messy bun. Makeup...eh. She didn't need makeup. Bella washed her face to remove the remnants of yesterday's makeup and ran out the door, completely forgetting her coat. But she was running so late that if she went back for her jacket and stopped for coffee plus a breakfast sandwich, Alicia might throw Bella's weighted down body into the ocean.

Seven o'clock in the morning meant the line at Steamy Beans Coffee Shop was out the door, and Bella was lucky to get in line only one storefront away. Bella adored having coffee across the street from the clinic. And not because Bella and Alicia didn't have a coffee maker. They did. Although they rarely had coffee on hand. Or snacks. Or time to make coffee.

She could see the clinic across the street from her spot in line, lights still off, blinds drawn. She beat Alicia. Kind of. The cost of victory was freezing her ass off.

Bella was all of two people lengths in the door, partially unthawing, when a newspaper dropped in front of her face, dulling the rich aroma of freshly brewed coffee.

'Is this the return of the social media starlet, Bella Astor?'

So, throwing that drink on Preston wasn't some horrendous nightmare?

Quickly scanning the article, Bella noted there wasn't a single word about the award. Thank you, New York Daily Life and Style section, for reporting about the entire night!

Her mother must be going absolutely ape shit. There was no way Lina hadn't read the paper yet. Bella hadn't looked at her phone since turning off the alarms. If her mother hadn't started yet, Lina Astor was sure to blow up her phone and thoroughly chew Bella out for this headline.

"I'm torn. I wish I had been there to see this in person and yet am sooooo glad I stayed at the Levvy," Alicia said. She shook off the pissed off patrons, jostling her full travel mug of coffee at them and popping the back of her tight mess of kinky black curls. Alicia has always been a damn morning person. With her radiant dark skin glistening and perfect makeup. She'd probably even showered. Absolutely disgusting how beautiful her other bestie was. How was she so perky this early in the day?

"Page five. Middle of the section. At least it's not the cover." Bella mumbled to herself. Maybe Mother missed the story itself. Bella's pocket vibrated. Scratch that. Her mother didn't miss a beat. Another buzz. Short enough, she was sure they were texts. She weighed the pros and cons of blocking her mother's cell number for the day. But blocking might prompt an in-person visit, though.

"Girl, you're on the cover of plenty."

Damn.

There were only a handful of newsstands near her apartment or the clinic, and Bella didn't remember passing any of them.

Alicia read her friend's face. "The Enquirer had the best picture." From the folds of the rest of the NY Daily, Alicia pulled the colored spread. Bella's elf dress enlarged, a blurry hand throwing the glass. "Now, let's not forget —"

Bella interrupted, saying, "We don't need to talk about social media. Period."

That was the actual issue. Papers Bella could forget about. Print wasn't completely dead, but Bella could manage if it was only there. Social media? For all she knew, a picture from the gallery would live on for years as a meme.

Check infamy off her list. If she hadn't already earlier in life. Soon someone might accuse her of staying in the limelight with stunts like this, just like other socialites making and their 'television careers.'

"I still have alerts for your name and hashtag." Alicia chewed on the inside of her cheek. "It's not pretty."

"The asshole didn't have the balls to dump me! He cheated on me. Why does no one remember that?"

"Yeah, they don't care, Bells. Preston's got this insane following now. No one cares that he's a douche." Alicia's eyes got that dreamy look she always got when ogling a boy. "God, look at that sexy, chiseled face. Was he still all toned under that..."

"Stop it!" Bella snarled. "I'm too under-caffeinated for this disgusting conversation. Your husband freaking modeled in Italy, and you're falling all over Preston again?" Something was seriously wrong with her best friend. Like, yea, Preston Warren was drop-dead gorgeous. He'd always been pretty. So pretty, the other guys never gave him crap for his beauty and instead fought over being his friend just to pick up his leftover women.

"There's a hierarchy of hot guys I know. And number one —"

"— is repellent? Repulsive?" Bella thought for a moment and added, "Repugnant?" Only the tip of the iceberg in describing Pres.

"Are you on Google looking up synonyms?"

Bella lifted her mostly empty hands besides the Life and Style section.

"You and those stupid crosswords. You're a freaking human thesaurus."

Sure, blame crossword puzzles, BFF, Bella thought.

"Anyway," Alicia continued, "One: Preston Warren. Two: Giovanni. Three —"

"Wait, Christian isn't two? He used to be."

Of course, Alicia's husband should be number one, but Alicia used to pine hard after Bella's twin brother.

"Remember when you said G modeled in Italy? Like five seconds ago."

If the line moved faster, she wouldn't have to hear this crap. Even answering her phone if Mother called became tempting.

Bella bit the bullet and asked, "Who's three?"

"Three: Chris. Four: Lucas."

"*Lucas?*" Bella started choking on nothing.

Alicia whistled. "He looks like a golden-haired prince from a freaking princess movie now. The man really grew into that chin, and those dimples are to die for, and, girl, Lucas filled out. Plus those suits he wears now. Ugh." Alicia fanned herself dramatically.

"I might need to call in sick. Not sure I can work under these conditions," Bella said as they inched forward.

Actually, Bella didn't disagree. She'd thought the same about Lucas and his suit last night. But it was weird hearing those thoughts from Alicia. Lucas never seemed to be on Alicia's radar in that capacity. Lucas was their best friend.

Alicia pinched her. "I still don't understand why you couldn't make it work," Alica sighed dreamily, Preston's picture in the Enquirer.

"The lying and cheating were extra charming." Bella pleaded silently, *Can't this line move any faster?*

"I would have worked around that." Cue more drooling by Alicia at the front page of the Enquirer.

Bella considered snatching the paper, rolling up, and smacking her bestie.

"I'm sorry," Alicia whined. "He's so hot, though." Bella gave her bestie her best channel-your-inner-teenager eye roll, and Alicia changed the subject. "I heard Warren's been pining away for you since we left."

The subject didn't change far enough. Bella's head throbbed.

"Funny way of showing it," Bella said.

Finally at the front of the line, Bella ordered a latte with an extra shot. She contemplated what level of fatty food would make Bella withstand dealing with her mother. Lina was going to find a way to cuss Bella out for having to do 'damage control.' And Alicia's constant and disgusting drooling over her ex-boyfriend (and possibly her brother if time allowed) added to the pain. She settled on a bacon egg croissant. Extra cheese.

"The asshole cheated on me. With my brother's fiancée."

"Cold feet?" Alicia asked, trying to play off the comment and ignore the deep hole she'd dug. Five seconds later, Alicia glanced at Bella and broke down. "Fine. You know my weakness is that hot douchebag. Whatever. So?"

Bella knew what Alicia was going to ask and preemptively hated it. She snatched her sandwich from the barista at the end of the counter and shoved the scalding hot breakfast sandwich in her mouth.

"Did you take anyone to the award shindig last night?"

Mouth full, Bella said, "You were thirty feet from when Daniel ambushed me. I mortified him, my brother, Lucas, and, most importantly, my mother just by wearing the elf costume."

"I thought Daniel would have had a change of clothes for you."

Daniel came prepared with a rack worth of dresses carefully laid out on the seat next to her. When Daniel asked if she'd chosen a suitable dress, Bella flat out lied.

"Ok, why didn't you just ask Lucas?"

This time she choked on actual food instead of just air.

"Why would I ask Lucas?" Bella said with a cough.

"I don't know. He's always there." Alicia pulled a piece of egg dangling from Bella's mouth. "He'd be an excellent date."

A smirk played on Alicia's glossy lips then she disappeared towards the exit, pushing and shoving her way through to the tail of the line amid some protests. On the sidewalk, Alicia stopped, speechless for once. Bella came out mostly unscathed, only a burned mouth from her attempt to deflect questions with the sandwich and a tiny coffee spill on her hand. Where they stood, they had a clear view of their clinic. Hope Clinic was short and squat compared to the surrounding buildings, with two large paned windows around the glass door and hand-painted lettering across each with the name, hours, and more. The blinds were still drawn closed since Alicia detoured to annoy Bella first.

Standing in front of their door was a man in a navy blue with salt and pepper hair, the onset of deeper wrinkles cut in around his cheeks. Next to him sat a massive paper-covered display. Bella recognized the shape.

Oh, no. Not today was he pulling that crap.

Squinting at their clinic, Alicia asked, "Is that in front of the —"

"— clinic." Bella finished. She unloaded her coffee and sandwich into Alicia's already full hands. She ran across the street, not even stopping to check for traffic. They'd stop for her, or she'd be spared having to be pissed off.

The delivery man in question saw Bella crossing. He dipped his head and moved down the street to a waiting Lexus SUV. Wow, low-end vehicle, if that was who she thought it was.

"Jackson! Jackson, you get back here!" Bella demanded Preston's assistant return immediately. "God damn it, Jackson." Her chest knotted.

Alicia made it across with only two cars blaring their horns at her and throwing curses out the window.

"What is it?" Using a single free finger, Alicia pulled at the paper to peek inside.

Less tactfully, Bella ripped the paper into large sections revealing, at minimum, twelve dozen velvety, overly fragrant red roses in a glass vase. Gasps reached them over the honking in the street.

"Holy shit." Both coffee cups and newspapers tumbled out of Alicia's hands. She'd only kept hold of Bella's precious sandwich. "What are you doing?" Alicia asked.

"It's blocking the doorway," Bella said.

Twelve dozen roses and the accompanying vase were much heavier than they looked. Bella bent and wrapped her hands around the vase, grunted with the effort of lifting them. Traffic stopped for Bella as she waddled back across the street. The vase almost slipped out of her hands, and she barely made it to the snow-covered bistro table that held the open sign for the coffee shop.

People in line immediately started asking for roses. Which worked out swimmingly for her. Bella took a few roses, handing them to patrons while pushing past to the front of the line.

She grabbed the first barista, not in the middle of drink making, explained about the vase and the flowers, and was prepared to beg for them to take the damn things off her hands. Hell, she'd even offer to post about it on whatever social media accounts she still had her passwords to if they let her leave them outside.

Steamy Beans' manager overheard and agreed so quickly Bella didn't even need to be the one to make a post. They were already in the middle of making a sign, 'Free Roses,' and composing a social media post.

When Bella returned with fresh coffee for her and Alicia, bought by a patron that took three roses for his three little girls. Then she plucked the clinic keys from Alicia's full hands and unlocked the clinic door.

"What?" Bella asked.

"I want to know what that man, or any man, needs to do to satisfy you."

Bella ignored her friend and took back her breakfast sandwich. No doubt this would be a long, stressful day, and all she'd had was a bacon, egg, and cheese sandwich. Maybe Bella could get something delivered at lunch.

However, as soon as she sat at their front desk and began reviewing the schedule, Bella knew that, like every day, it was a packed day. No time for lunch. A wet card fell on top of the schedule book. Alicia gave her a wry grin.

You owe me for dry cleaning. ~Pres

Bella crushed the card in her hand. That conniving, pretentious, pompous, petty (the alliteration could go on for Preston)...*she owes him* for dry cleaning?

Her phone buzzed again, longer this time. A phone call. Bella pushed her mother to voicemail and struggled to remember why she'd come back from Frontier Doctors.

Lucas

"Why are you home this morning?" Chris stood blocking the door of Lucas' condo. Not that Lucas was trying to leave. He was standing in the brilliantly white kitchen. Half the lights off to allow him to adjust to all the morning light his unforgiving floor-to-ceiling windows provided even with the blinds closed. Lucas stared at his friend, coffee pot poised over his chipped Kalamazoo Central High School alumnus mug. Steam fogged Lucas' wire-rimmed glasses as Chris crossed to the counter, leaving the front door dangling open to the elegant hallway. The site of the matched tones of cream and grainy light wood edged with a dark gray tile through the dangling open door still unsettled Lucas.

But it was a bonus to Chris owning the entire floor with only two occupants. No one except Chris could randomly walk into his apartment. The elevator required a code to access their floor.

Chris helped himself to a mug and held it out for Lucas to fill.

Lucas said, "I do live here." He poured the other half of the carafe into Chris' mug.

Sometimes. Admittedly, Lucas spent most nights at Bella's apartment in Astoria.

Shoes, or something just as hard, hit the floor across the hall. Chris walked over and shut Lucas' door with an almost inaudible click.

Ah. Lucas grinned at Chris. *Someone* was hiding from a woman.

Grabbing the sugar and cream, Lucas dulled the bitterness of the cheap coffee and guessed, "Server from last night?"

Chris sipped the coffee and blanched. "I'm bringing over different coffee tonight. This is abysmal."

"Then don't drink it."

Despite his decent salary, Lucas didn't spend like he had no worries. He kept to a budget for everything. Clothes, food, his car. The only reason he even lived in Central Park West was Chris couldn't live alone when Bella made plans to join Frontier Doctors. The man literally bought out a multi-million dollar floor like it was nothing (Lucas suspected Chris' father, Eli Astor, had a helping hand in the deal, but he couldn't be sure) and gave Lucas the condo across the hall at a ridiculous steal. Lucas insisted on paying rent even if it was a pittance. Didn't matter. With Chris' twin gone, he needed a friend close by. It was Chris' way of admitting he missed his sister.

He'd even set aside a whole other condo for his sister and a spare as a 'guest house,' but Bella refused the offer when she came home.

"Damage control notwithstanding, last night went better than I thought it might," Chris said and ripped a banana from the bunch sitting on the counter.

"Did you not check your phone this morning?" Lucas grabbed eggs and bread from the fridge. The refrigerator door slammed shut, its paneling making it blend in with the rest of the cabinets. Lucas hated that whole aesthetic. In his opinion, a fridge should look like a fridge.

Turning, Lucas found Chris grimacing into his coffee. Chris asked, "What happened now?"

Daniel had been messaging Lucas since he'd woken. Mystically, the man knew exactly when Lucas woke and texted approximately three minutes after warning him Lina Astor was on the warpath.

After Daniel's initial messages, Lucas looked at Twitter. Then Instagram. Then...he couldn't look anymore.

Alicia texted him pictures of the New York Daily and the Enquirer while she'd been waiting at a crosswalk.

"I should have confirmed, but I would have assumed Mr. Emile Warren Esquire would have attended last night. Not Pres." Chris said. His frown deepened as he drank the coffee.

Lucas' phone rattled on the counter at the same time as Chris', interrupting Lucas from whipping his eggs. A text from Alicia.

Alicia: Preston sent flowers?!?!?!

Then came a string of puke emojis followed.

"Huh," Chris murmured to himself.

"What?"

Chris relished the moment with a sip of coffee, even if it was stale cheap coffee, and said, "Well, I mean...we knew Pres had more balls than you."

"This again?" Lucas didn't really want to hear it. Bella was beyond pissed off. After she got the plaque, they ducked out to his car, and he brought her back to the screening event at Levvy Rec Center, which they found locked up. The event was over. They must have driven through a dead zone and missed Alicia's text, letting them know there was no point returning.

So, Lucas called for pizza, timing it so they would get back to Bella's apartment with beer and meet the delivery driver, which was perfect.

Until they opened the box, and they'd received the wrong pizza. The beer combined with banana curry pizza did not sit well.

Bella agreed to a reset. Give up on the night, huddle in bed, and try again tomorrow. He couldn't disagree with her. He wanted the day over, too. Lucas pecked her forehead, melted at those big brown eyes, and ultimately drove home.

Another text interrupted Lucas' daydreaming about Bella's soft peck on his forehead.

A picture of a card with: *You owe me for dry cleaning. ~Pres*

Lucas gaped at his phone but now felt a bit more at ease, then turned on the burner under his frying pan. He added a pat of butter and dumped the eggs in too early, half the butter still unmelted.

"Yes, Preston Warren has balls." Smugness crept into his tone, adding, "That Bella is going to crush."

"You know, despite the fact that Bella is insane and probably will kick his ass for that card," Chris opened the same text, shaking his head. "Pres knows what he's doing. Getting under Bella's skin means she's thinking about him."

"What are you saying?" Lucas looked away from his over scrambled eggs. "Bella doesn't think about me?"

"No. She does. You're just," Chris' voice dropped lower, "friend zoned."

Yes. Lucas was friend zoned, and he didn't have anyone to blame but himself. After years of trying to tell Bella how he felt, he could never get the words to come out. He vowed he would do it and willed himself to practice. But, she'd look at him, cock her head to the side and beam or throw her legs over his lap and snuggle in. Lucas was transported back to freshman year at Columbia when he couldn't form single-word responses to Bella.

Since he entered her hospital room at Central Clinic of Athens, 28 hours after the explosion in Syria last year, Lucas thought he'd worked past his anxiety about his feelings.

For weeks, they did everything together. Lucas helped her shower, which was a feat with his eyes squeezed shut. He took her to all her rehab appointments and follow-ups. Two whole weeks of cooking her breakfast, lunch, and dinner for her. Practically living in her tiny new apartment in Astoria, stopping at home only to change his suit for the few hours of work.

Nope. Apparently, all that time together had the opposite effect. What if telling Bella his feelings ruined what they had?

Chris and Alicia both agreed he was being ridiculous. And it wasn't like he'd given up trying to figure out how to tell Bella his feelings. The strategy for telling Bella and not messing up just wasn't coming to him, so he used a lot of excuses like 'it's not a good time' to stall. Of course, his friends all countered with, 'it's never going to be a good time.'

Chris came around the island and shut off the burner under Lucas' overdone eggs. "I, personally, don't think you should be friend zoned. Not with the way you love Bells. Ok? You both deserve that happiness together."

Says the guy that rarely took a woman on a second date. At least, not anymore.

CHAPTER SIX
Food is the way to a woman's heart

Bella

Bella's mind wandered to bear claws, danishes, anything gooey and sticky and sweet and...

Stop! She shouted at herself.

A pinch of pain shot across her shoulder, breaking the sugary spell from Steamy Beans wafting in as the door closed again. The coffee shop was a beacon of hope and wakefulness in the morning. However, in the afternoon, Steamy Beans haunted her with decadent pastry and coffee scents carried in each time a patient entered the clinic. She'd only been sitting for a minute when her stomach growled angrily. One more patient. Bella weighed if she had time to run across the street to grab anything.

After a day of torturing her via texts from the next exam room and annoying notes on every sticky note they owned, Alicia left during Bella's second to last appointment. She quickly knocked on Bella's exam room door to let her know she was on her way out.

Bella meant to beg her friend to run across and grab something for Bella to eat but was in the middle of explaining medication to her patient and couldn't stop.

When that patient left, Bella found yet another hot pink sticky note screaming at her on top of the schedule to 'BUY SNACKS ALREADY, B!'.

Huh. The mystery of the empty snack drawer was solved! Bella's turn, and she forgot, just like she forgot to buy her own groceries. She'd really been off lately. Lately being a relative term. 'Lately' as in since she returned home to New York nearly eight months prior. She thought coming home would be easier than it had been. Sure, adjusting would take time, but she'd get back to her normal routine, and everything would fall back into place. Boy, was she wrong. Before Frontier Doctors, Bella was constantly on top of every part of her life. Fully stocked kitchen, meals, exercise, school work, or her residency. She was so on top of her life that Bella outshone her brother. At one point, her father considered placing Bella as CEO of Astor Pharm instead of Chris. Now she couldn't remember to get basic necessities.

The ting-a-ling of the bell on the front door jolted Bella. In came her last client, a sweet brunette woman named Melissa.

And that answered Bella's burning question. No, she did not have time to run across to Steamy Beans for coffee or a snack.

Bella hid her disappointment behind paperwork for Melissa and busied herself forming questions for her new client. Melissa echoed Bella's own fatigue. Messy ponytail falling low after a day of work. The woman's uniform from one of the chain stores.

Melissa's exam didn't take long. An injury from overworking. Everything would have gone faster if Melissa had checked her unnerving stare at the door.

Eventually, near the end of the exam, while Bella was making notes on Melissa's chart, her patient said, "I know you," in that slow, deliberate way. Like she was thinking very hard over Bella's face.

After someone said things like, 'I know you,' it took a few extra moments to come to people. Even with Bella's ID swinging around her neck, her full name in plain sight. No one ever looked at the nametag before saying, ' I know you.'

To move the process along, Bella fiddled with the plastic tag and impatiently twisted a lock of messy blond hair that had fallen from her bun.

"No way!" Melissa exclaimed.

Ah, annoying recognition.

"You're not like *the* Bella Astor, are you?"

Melissa's eyes widened like a cartoon. Bella was used to that, too. No one seemed to think Bella looked much like '*the* Bella Astor' plastered across tabloids. Or from that video from high school...

Gurgle.

Great interruption.

Melissa stopped and made a face at Bella and her obnoxious 'can't-leave-well-enough-alone-yes-she-knew-that-she-hadn't-eaten-since-7-AM' stomach.

"I didn't eat lunch," Bella said, waiting for the doctor's note to print. Another louder groan echoed from her stomach, and Bella added, "Or dinner."

"You're *the* Bella Astor?" Melissa reiterated. "Oh, my god! You tried to stab Preston Warren."

Good God! Where the hell did people hear this stuff?

"It was a glass. And if I wanted to hit Pres, I would have." Bella tried to keep the comment under her breath.

Really, Bella tried to be pleasant as she escorted Melissa back out of her exam room. She'd pressed the letter into the woman's hand with the summary from her visit. They were barely out the door when Melissa full-on stopped. Bella crashed into her patient's back, and they both caught themselves on the front desk.

Melissa righted herself. She fixed her hair obsessively and adjusted her hunter green work polo while staring at Lucas's slightly unkempt blond hair and muscular physique. The man was stopping traffic, literally, with those rolled-up shirtsleeves.

Lucas crushed Melissa's wistful dreams almost immediately when he started singing. "Fa la la la la," came out adorably and purposely off key, a nail protruding from between his teeth.

"You didn't find that funny yesterday," Bella snapped playfully.

Marking the location for the plaque, Lucas got the nail ready and said, "No, I didn't. Brought you dinner, Bells."

Lucas tilted his head at a plain white plastic bag tied closed. Her stomach grumbled so loudly Lucas couldn't help but chuckle.

"Have a good night," he said, his deep baritone nearly taking out Melissa's knees.

Lucas glanced at Bella as she mouthed 'thank you.'

It took Lucas setting down his hammer and holding the door open for Melissa to cross the reception room in a flurry of giggles and preening. The door shut, and Bella collapsed into the closest chair.

"You're both a godsend and a hazard." Bella massaged the migraine forming at her temples.

"Hazard? Pretty sure I just saved you. And you *hate* when a guy 'saves you.'"

"I only allow you to 'save me' because I know I can hand you your ass on the mat."

"Touché."

Bella scrubbed her face, stopping to remember if she'd put makeup on that morning. Preston's dumb flowers and dumb gestures, and dumb...self made Bella scream through her hands.

Lucas lined up the nail again and paused, hammer held back. "Dinner?"

Bella finally mumbled through her fingers, "I can't believe you bought me dinner."

"I mean," Lucas grinned and continued, "If it counts as saving you again, I could eat it."

"No!" she said and seized the bag before he could, even jokingly, reach down to grab it.

Oh lord, the bag smelled heavenly. Sharp and smooth hints of cheese tickled her nose. "You didn't." Bella sighed contentedly after another inhale.

"Straight from Sek'end Sun."

She caught the gleam in Lucas' eye and smiled even brighter. Bella *loved* Sek'end Sun; nothing could beat their mac and cheese fresh out of the oven. But Lucas had to drive out of his way an extra eight blocks to stop and get her favorite dish before backtracking to the clinic.

Bella pulled out the container, still radiating heat, and felt herself get as gooey as the cheesy pasta inside.

"How does it look?" Lucas asked. When his eyes settled, a smirk settled as well. He pointed at the cheese dripping from the side of her mouth.

But Bella wasn't focused on the plaque. She was focused on how almost five years had done wonders to Lucas that she couldn't tell over video chat. Usually, she only saw his face and hair covered in a baseball cap or bandana.

Back when they met, Lucas was still slim, but recently he'd filled out with more muscle tone. He'd become wider in the hips and chest with broad, round shoulders. His jawline cemented itself, and the cleft in his chin that had been cute as a dimple before became a memorable, pretty damn sexy feature. And his smile included delectable dimples.

Literally, none of this was what Lucas was talking about. He looked from the plaque to her and back again.

Damn it. What was she thinking? This was all Alicia's fault! Her partner's weird conversation earlier infiltrated her brain, making Bella think about Lucas!

Looking up, Bella saw the plaque hanging handsomely between the watercolor paintings Giovanni gifted to their clinic from his hometown, Florence, Italy.

She slurped down what noodles and cheese were in her mouth without choking and said, "Just where I was going to hang it."

Lucas' expression softened, and he chewed his lips. A buzz rattled the keys in his pocket. And somehow, Lucas utterly ignored his phone.

Heat rose into Bella's cheeks as Lucas watched her while she ate, ignoring his phone when it buzzed again.

Both jumped when the clinic's bell rang as someone opened the door.

"We're closed," Bella and Lucas said in unison, and why were her cheeks and ears so freaking hot?

"You should answer that." Preston's cool voice threw proverbial ice water onto Bella. Then, with the barest threads of civility, Preston added, "Mr. Holt."

"Mr. Warren," Lucas said in equally frigid tones.

"I came to have a word with Bella."

"Do you mean Dr. Astor?" Lucas stepped between them, chin held high, trying to make up the few inches he was shorter than Pres. "Maybe you should have phoned ahead. Made an appointment."

Preston leered down at Lucas, "I thought Hope Clinic took walk-ins."

"Oh, good God." Bella rocked herself out of the chair. "We're not measuring...egos here, boys."

Preston, though, couldn't drop the competition. "I'd win."

To keep from hurling herself at Preston, Bella looped her arm through Lucas', gripped his bicep, and said, "That's not necessarily the case."

Eyes widened in surprise, Preston asked, "Like you'd know, Bells?"

"Pretty sure my 'ego' is biggest," she sneered. "Now get the hell out of my clinic."

Lucas flushed, and Preston's grin grew wider.

"I'll bet your 'ego' is." He turned just enough to prove he was excluding Lucas, then Preston said, "I just want to talk, Bells. Explain."

Bella hesitated, unsure how to answer. For most of her life, Bella stood up for Preston through all his crappy behavior. She'd fed herself the bullshit line, *'that's how Pres always treated women and was just how things worked in their corner of society,'* over and over until she believed the lie too. He was her best friend, and Bella would listen to whatever Preston had to say because he was Preston, a guy she grew up loving. Granted, she knew how terribly Pres treated people by college, but he was still her friend.

Until he became the guy that broke Bella Astor.

Lucas answered for her, "She doesn't want you here."

"Bella can make that..."

Bella said, "I don't want you here." The words felt stale. Almost like she wasn't sure. But it was Preston. *He cheated on your ass with Chris' fiancé, so there's no point in hearing him out!* Sweet, beautiful logic.

"That doesn't sound very confident. Five minutes." Preston rubbed his jaw, the stubble long enough that it jutted out at various angles after each fidget. "Please, Bells. All I want is a *private* conversation."

The way Preston leveled his annoyingly velvety dark brown eyes on Lucas, Bella was glad she still had a hold of him. She would not blame Lucas if he lunged for Preston's throat.

Lucas squeezed the handle of the hammer until Bella slid her hand over his, feeling the tension ebb. "It's fine."

Clearly, Lucas didn't buy it; his jaw squared.

"Run along, Holt." Preston waved at the door. Bella half expected one of the Warren attendants to be waiting and open the door to ensure Lucas left the premises.

Lucas' arm tensed under hers. He leaned down and whispered, "What do you want to do? I can take you home right now."

As much as it pained her, Bella knew she *should* hear Preston out, a first step to smoothing things over with her mother after the debacle at the award ceremony last night. Show that she's "making an effort" or whatever.

"Bella?" Lucas pushed himself between Bella and Preston, concern written across his face.

"Might get the ice queen off my case. I can't believe I'm in my 30s and worrying about that."

"You're sure?" Lucas rightly asked because *he* did *not* look sure.

"I'll be fine."

A total and complete lie. But Bella could absolutely fake being okay until she was safely holed up in her apartment again.

"You heard her," Preston said, then nudged Lucas. "She'll be fine. She's a big girl."

Finally breaking his hold on Bella's arm, Lucas spun on Preston again. "She's not a girl. She's a woman. Has been for a very long time."

"And Bella said she wants to speak with me. This is private, so you can see yourself out now."

Electricity charged the air around all the guys. To break the spell, Bella stood on tiptoes, dared to grab Lucas around his chest, and settled her chin on his shoulder. Preston absolutely seethed at them.

She whispered, "I'll call you later."

What possessed Bella to peck Lucas on the cheek, she could not say. But the absolute horror on Preston's face was both palpable and gratifying.

Lucas leaned back into Bella, a renewed smirk on his face. He was refusing to break Preston's glare. Preston nodded again at the door. Reluctantly, Lucas broke Bella's grasp, and she felt unsteady without him pressing into her. But like always, he caught her shoulders and kept her on her feet.

"Are you sure?" Lucas' crystal blue eyes searched hers.

"Yeah," Bella said. Though her thoughts were more like, *No! Stay, or take me with you! Don't leave me.*

Brushing her hair behind her ear sent a shiver down her spine.

Lucas said, "I'm a text away."

Bella nodded. A text away.

Before leaving, Lucas dropped the hammer on a coffee table and plucked his suit jacket from the chair he'd draped it on. Not bothering to put the jacket on, Lucas tossed it over his shoulder and, an instant later was out the door.

The door jingled shut, leaving behind a thick silence.

"Well, he's still sniffing around, eh? Pathetic." Preston chuckled.

Bella tried to draw in a calming breath through locked teeth. "What do you want, Preston?"

"You got my gift." This wasn't a question. Jackson obviously reported that he'd delivered the flowers.

With a fold of her arms, Bella tapped her foot faster and faster until Preston continued on his own.

"It's so weird. I'm not sure I've seen a woman eat a carb in public in years."

"Thought you wanted to explain?"

Somehow, the way Pres thoughtfully rubbed his jaw, fingers playing happily with his stubble, irritated Bella down to her core.

"Yes. But first, you owe me for—"

Her hand crashed into the mac and cheese, flinging a handful at Preston's precious fucking Armani suit.

"I owe you?" Bella squealed. "What the fuck do I owe you, Preston? I owe you nothing! I-I...get out! Either explain yourself or get the hell out of my clinic!"

Never mind. Bella thought she could talk with Pres. No, she definitely could not even hear him out. Cocky, smug, son of a bitch! Did he think she'd fall into line like every other woman he'd ever dealt with?

In a rare moment, Preston was speechless, wiping clumped macaroni onto the clinic floor.

Then he said, "Again?"

"You're right! I think you deserve a hell of a lot more!" She moved to grab another handful, and Pres jumped to stop her.

"Okay. Okay."

Jumping across the room, Preston grabbed and held her wrist. Her hand was full of mac and cheese, and he asked, "Can we call a truce?"

Damn the fact that he smelled so good. Just a hint of his signature cologne still left from the morning clung to his suit. And his soft hands holding her wrist.

Remember the anger. Remember why Preston was an ass.

Trish and Pres in bed together. Her bed.

Okay. That did it.

"I don't know. Can you possibly not ruin people's lives?" Rage in her burned so hotly and deeply that Bella felt ill. She wrestled from Preston's grasp and wiped her hand on her scrubs.

"Fine. If you won't explain, get the hell out." She shoved Pres towards the door. "Or you won't only be wearing mac and cheese!"

"Bella!" Preston tried to stop her, his hands grabbing hold of her shoulders.

Which set her off even more. Bella tore away and went straight for the noodles again, whipping another handful at him. "Five years, Preston! Five! Not one apology! Not a single attempt to...argh! If you cared so much—why?"

"Bella? Can we talk *without* food?"

"I can't do this tonight. Out." Her eyes stung with fresh tears.

Grabbing his jacket sleeve, Bella dragged him to the door, shoved him out, and pulled out her keys. Her voice trembled as she said, "My humiliation wasn't enough? What? You need to revel in it further?"

"Bells?"

No! God damn it! Lucas could call her that. Chris. Alicia. Pres' right to that name was revoked.

"I'm going home."

If Bella didn't look, he couldn't try to smolder his way into her fucking good graces again.

"Bells?" He dangled keys in her face. "Bella. Please, I just want to talk. You don't need to walk. I can drive you home, and we can..."

"Talk? You want to talk? Okay, talk! Tell me: was that night the first time you slept with Trish, or was I just some running gag at all the Astor galas you were my date to, and you snuck off with her at each one? I have been waiting for almost five years for an actual explanation."

"Bells, that's not fair. I tried..."

"Yes! Sorry. You tried. At my father's funeral! Not exactly an appropriate place to explain why you cheated on me!"

"Bella...I wanted to apologize...I guess it wasn't the best timing."

Behind her, a car door clicked open. Bella wheeled around to yell but saw Lucas leaning against the hood of his faded red beat to hell fifteen-year-old Corolla, holding the door open. He left the door hanging, walked over, and wrapped his suit jacket over her shoulders.

"Holt! I'm trying to have a private conversation."

"That was private?" Lucas tilted his head to Steamy Beans, where teens sipped coffee well past when Bella could drink a caffeinated drink and not be up all night. They all had their phones out.

Lucas continued, "You and I have very different definitions of the word private."

Bella tilted her head to the gloomy, gray sky overhead, lit with New York's ambient glow, blinking away tears.

"Need a ride?" This time, Bella turned and found Lucas' smile wasn't full of venom or malice toward Preston. Just empathy.

"Bella?" Preston tried once more, but she was determined not to listen.

"Not tonight, Pres."

Bella tightened the jacket around her shoulders, strode from the two men, and climbed into Lucas' car.

CHAPTER SEVEN

Ketchup is a perfectly normal condiment!

Lucas

Bella slouched in her seat, wrapping the jacket further around her arms, glared straight ahead, and avoided looking at Preston.

Lucas carefully shut the door, and though the night's brisk wind cut straight through his dress shirt, Lucas gave Preston one last grin and a mock two-fingered salute. Preston seethed, eyes locked on Lucas as he walked around his beat-to-hell car.

Worth it.

Chris' comment from that morning, *She's thinking about him*, kept echoing in the back of his mind. Yeah, she was thinking about Preston but sitting next to Bella now, he saw her eyes well up and her lip tremble. Lucas' stomach churned. Sure, Bella thought about Preston, which was tearing Bella apart when she did.

"Just drive," Bella moaned, sliding low in her seat to become invisible.

"Home?" Lucas asked after pulling out of the parking space and into the relatively (in New York standards) light post-rush hour traffic.

Bella curled in on herself and made weird twisted faces at the dashboard while mumbling under her breath. As close to a yes as he was going to get. As they passed under streetlights, he saw the blotchy red patches on her cheeks grow brighter, then she turned a bit green, clutching her stomach.

Lucas let a comfortable silence settle between them.

Years of being best friends, and he'd only seen her cry a handful of times before coming home from Frontier Doctors. And countless more crying sessions since returning home.

After circling her block several times, Lucas found a parking spot up the street from Bella's building and shut off the car. He turned and stared at Bella, still making faces at the dashboard.

"Bella?"

Lucas waved his hand in front of her face, trying to snap her out of her stupor. She didn't react. He did it again and again, each pass getting closer and closer to her nose until he...*boop*!

Bella jumped a foot out of her skin. "What?" She squealed and smacked him.

Which stung. A lot. But he hid the wince and jutted his chin at her building down the street. "Home," he said and ruffled her hair.

She heaved a huge, heavy sigh. Lucas got out, and even when he came around, she still hadn't opened the passenger door.

"Come on," Lucas said, knocking on the window.

Bella blatantly refused to move. Slouching further in the passenger seat.

"Bella?"

Lucas opened the door and stared long and hard at her. He was actually tired, and his eyes itched terribly from too long in his contacts. Balling his fists, he stopped himself from rubbing his eyes. Bella stayed slumped in the passenger seat, resolute in staring straight ahead.

Fine. Lucas pulled both of her hands, hoping all she needed was a slight push to move. But she sat there.

Lucas repeated, "Come on."

Fissures formed in her Preston-induced bad mood. Bella glared at him, a grin hiding behind her sour face.

Lucas gave her one more shot. "I'll do it."

Thank God for the dark night and not being under a street-light. His cheeks burned hot, but Lucas followed through on the threat. It always, without a doubt, made her smile. He bent, snatching Bella's waist, and lifted her out of the car onto his shoulder.

"Lucas!" Bella squealed. Legs flailing wildly. "Put me down!"

A sharp poke hit him between the ribs. His arms hopped off Bella's legs for a moment. She let out a sharp yelp, and he grabbed hold again before she fell.

"Truce?"

He tried to turn and see her, but all that was there was...her...no. Lucas bent and set her down on the sidewalk, Bella still full of giggles.

"Truce," she agreed.

"Better?" Lucas asked.

She jabbed his shoulder. Bella caught the suit jacket before it fell and said, "Better."

Lucas stopped to adjust the jacket to fit her better. His fingers lingered at her shoulders. The way she played with her lip, chewing on it, turned every last thought of his to mush.

"You coming up?" Bella broke through the mushy state.

"Pfft. Of course," Lucas said, stuttering on each word. He recovered poorly from his stupor.

Bella always asked, without fail, if Lucas wanted to come up. And Lucas never said no. Especially when she'd been crying. Her eyes were already glassy again, a new threat of tears rearing its ugly head.

Bells turned out of his grasp and forced herself to appear chipper, skip-hopping to the door of her building.

Lucas looked up at the line of tall windows embedded in the red brick building above the door. Bella's building was older, single pane windows dripped with condensation clinging to the glass, lit by multicolored Christmas trees near the windows.

Inside the front door, Bella released his suit jacket only long enough to retrieve her mail from the wall of locked metal boxes and gasped, "OOOH, I may have just won $10,000."

He took the sweepstakes letter and tapped her head the rest of the way up the stairs. In a series of jumps and dodges, they made their way through the dimly lit stairwell up to the third floor and Bella's apartment.

Over the last 24 hours, this was what was missing. This version of Bella. The world felt almost right again.

Lucas chuckled or ruffled her hair while she joked. Inevitably, her jokes hiccuped, and he saw it again. Preston's effect peeking through. They were at the third-floor landing when Bells gave up and sighed, and the jokes were done.

He hadn't even thought of which question, burning in the back of his mind, to ask. *What did Pres say? Are you okay? Can we file some legal documents or restraining order against him?*

But Bella preempted him with, "Don't bring it up," while she jabbed the key in her lock and wiggled it around. Eyes piercing into his soul in the same unsettling way her mom could.

Okay. Fine. He won't bring Preston up. But there was one other, tiny question bothering him. "Did you leave the mac and cheese at the clinic?"

A light dawned on her face, a mixture of mortification and depression.

"I mean...it went well with that suit," Lucas teased. That earned him a more brutal jab to the same shoulder from before. He pressed on, "I know nothing about color but —"

Third jab. That one hurt.

Bella began wrenching the key so violently he feared she'd break it off in the lock again. Lucas took over. In one swift move, he brought the key up and leaned in. The door gave.

Like many New York apartments, Bella's apartment reminded Lucas of a long closet. It was the exact opposite of his spacious, boxy apartment, the type of apartment an Astor should be living in.

They walked straight into the tiny living room. On cue, Bella's stomach groaned. Bella let out an agonizing moan. She flopped face first over the back of the couch right past the doorway, dragging his suit jacket over her head. Lucas ignored her and walked into her tiny kitchen. The small room consisted of a few cabinets, a breakfast bar, a sink, and a sliver of counter space for cooking next to her refrigerator and stove.

Through a door behind the kitchen, Bella's spare bedroom had been retrofitted to be a home gym but currently gathered dust.

"So," Lucas said as he glanced at the pile of limbs and cloth, "should I make you dinner?"

Bella mumbled into the pillow.

"I'll take that as a —" Lucas started as he swung the fridge door open and heaved his own sigh. "You have ketchup."

Bella appeared at the fridge door so quickly that Lucas jumped.

"It's a perfectly normal condiment to have in the fridge!"

Under normal circumstances, he would laugh at the joke and her fridge, but he was also hungry. His eyes were itching, almost burning, and he was as done with the day as Bella. He'd seen Preston Warren more times in two evenings than he'd seen him in the last six months. Particularly considering Preston was one of the legal councils for Astor Pharm.

Lucas said, "It's the only thing in your fridge!"

Her hand grabbed the door and pulled hard. "It's not..."

But the evidence was undeniable. There was nothing in Bella's fridge other than packets of ketchup. Not a bottle, but packets from takeout.

"What are you? My mother?"

"Don't compare me to your mother," Lucas replied. An icy shiver shook him to the bone.

Bella abandoned the joke. Her smile faded, and she lost focus on the conversation and the fridge.

Worried he would make whatever Bella was feeling worse, Lucas went back to searching her kitchen and overthinking what to say next.

She was out of everything. No rice, pasta, or canned vegetables. He searched through her pathetic excuse for a pantry, the freezer, even the cabinets over the fridge she couldn't reach without a chair. Nothing.

Sitting on the counter, Bella's eyes fixed on her Astor Pharm badge. She kept extending it out, then letting the badge snap back in.

He had to do something. This was torture watching Bella spiral.

"I missed a meeting today."

She looked up at him, and he coughed nervously. *Was this the right thing to bring up?*

Lucas balled up his fists again to keep from rubbing his eyes. He should have taken his contacts out at the office and thrown on his glasses. But he had to press on. Not scratch.

"Is this some bad joke?" Bells asked.

"No joke. Chris came looking for me." Chris thought Lucas had done something drastic after their talk that morning and was hiding in a corner in utter embarrassment. He *was* hiding in a corner somewhere in the building. More out of fear. "I think Daniel set me up on purpose."

"Twice in two days? That would be a record. Wait...what does Daniel have to do with you missing a meeting?"

"I had his phone and still can't figure out why or how. And then Lina called..."

"Oh, God!" Bells paused mid-pull on her badge. "You picked up a call from my mother?"

"I - well, in my defense - I thought it was my phone, and if your mother ever called my actual phone and I didn't pick up, I think I'd end up in the Hudson. I don't think it mattered. Pretty sure your mother thought I was Daniel. I couldn't get a word in edgewise."

"Couldn't? Or *couldn't*?" Bella said. Her badge snapped back to her belly. "You couldn't speak at all, could you?"

No. Exactly zero words were actually exchanged with Lina Astor during her tirade about the whole 'Preston Warren debacle.'

"Your mother can freezer burn souls. We're talking whole stadiums at a time. It's freaky."

There it was. Bella broke the bonds of Preston's influence over her. He just needed that hold to crack a little more.

"Does my torture amuse you, Dr. Astor?"

Dimple in the smile. There was his Bella.

"Nope," Bella said. Her smile widened, and her teeth showing through made his heart skip a beat. "It's nothing. Go put your glasses on. Spares are in the bathroom."

Lucas caught himself rubbing his eyes. Clearly, Bells saw it too.

But he wasn't done. "Classic deflection, Bells."

"God! You were talking to my mother!" She slapped his sore shoulder and said, "You've been clenching your hands. You don't want to rub your eyes. Go!"

Lucas scooped her off the counter, back onto his shoulder without preamble. She squealed again, battering his back playfully. He dropped her on the couch in a heap and moved to the bathroom, searching for his spare glasses.

Safely ensconced in her closet-sized bathroom, Lucas took out his spare contact case and solution from the medicine cabinet. His eyes burned, but he got the contacts out, then washed his face. Lucas was overheating. He couldn't do this.

Part of him took Chris' annoying talk that morning to heart. Preston was stuck in Bella's mind. Maybe it was time for him to tell her how he felt. See if she felt the same.

But Lucas ran through every scenario before, during, and after work. Most ended in Lucas losing Bells as a friend (either because she completely and utterly rejected him or broke up with him because they weren't compatible), his job, moving back in with his parents, and never working a managerial job ever again.

Actually, every scenario ended like that, eventually.

God, he could not tell her. What would Lucas be if he told her and they started dating? A rebound? Five years after the fact, but still...he'd be a rebound. He wouldn't be the rebound and lose her. And he certainly was not going to add to her emotional overload when Preston was busy freshly tearing open that wound he left with her.

No matter how much he wanted to finally tell her.

The door creaked open, Bella standing there in her rumpled scrubs, rumpled hair, bags under her eyes, holding out a cereal bar. Her eyes were red again; unlike her usual self, she stared at the bars in her hand. Not her head held high. Not exuding that Astor confidence in the face of everything.

"Found these in the cabinet."

"Let me guess," Lucas said. He dried his face. Pawing around for the glasses case, Bella beat him to it and handed them to him. "You rushed out this morning? Didn't even know you had these?"

"Nope. I..."

"You're a terrible liar." Lucas brought back Bells' old insult against him.

She lost that glow she got when she laughed for real and fiddled with the wrapper.

"Thank you," Bella said, wobbly voice and all.

He pulled her in for a hug, resting his chin on her head. "Any time." Damn the fact that the wobble was contagious.

"You look good, Holt," she teased. The same thing she always said when he put his glasses on, but this time into his chest. Her voice, though, was growing steadier again.

And that was enough for his cheeks to grow hot. Thankfully, she was tucked in and couldn't see his face.

CHAPTER EIGHT

Questions

Bella

Two boxes of cereal bars dropped into Bella's hand basket. Next to her, Lucas fumed. That! Those little things amused Bella enough to keep her moving.

During the drive to the Food Emporium, Bella had eight blissful minutes of rest. Blissful even considering she cussed out three drivers who'd cut off Lucas at three different intersections. Of course, most things were more relaxing than the shit show of the last few days.

"Ugh?" Clutching his chest, Lucas mocked her snack choice. "That's like torture! Why, Bells? Why?"

Her eyes locked on Lucas' as she tipped the third box into the basket.

"That's really insulting." Lucas pantomimed daggers in the heart, and she worked hard not to crack up. He said, "I make you breakfast all the time. Don't do it! Don't..."

And she tipped a fourth in. Now Lucas pressed his lips together in a tight line. Like, for real. Or as real as he could without laughing at her. "You're as bad as a cat. There was a time when you made me breakfast."

Ah, yes. Back in the good old college days, when Alicia assumed hanging out with Bella and Christian Astor would be all chauffeurs, chefs, maids, and parties. Instead, she was sorely disappointed. Yes, Bella had access to those and mostly was chauffeured around, but she rarely allowed for those other luxuries in her daily life (though Chris used to hide having a maid come in twice a week to clean their college apartment).

The tight line of Lucas' lips broke when he looked at her for too long, but he refused to smile.

Bella shrugged, saying. "We need snacks at the clinic. And I need Alicia not to kill me. Which *will* happen if I don't bring snacks tomorrow."

While digging through her basket of snack bars, cereal bars, and fruit cups (but packed in syrup and shelf stable and not exactly the healthiest thing), Lucas said, "It doesn't have to be crap like this. I doubt she said 'bring sugar and lots of it.'"

"This doesn't go bad," Bella said half-heartedly.

She was lazy. No, not lazy. Bella knew she was still having trouble adjusting to life back home. To cooking, cleaning... her natural rhythm wasn't natural anymore.

"Food in the clinic doesn't have time to go bad. At least get some fruit." He plucked a bunch of bananas from his basket and dropped them in hers. "And bring leftovers for lunch."

"Can't." Bella forced her voice to sing.

Honestly, she would bring leftovers. But in her sleep and caffeine deprived state, she either forgot they existed or forged during sleepless nights when Lucas slept in his own apartment.

And many times when they ate together, there were no leftovers.

She was about to tip a fifth box in, purely out of spite, except Lucas sucked the joy out by stomping away, although his head and shoulders were shaking. She was pretty sure he was laughing at her and not in a rage cursing her very existence. Maybe 70% sure, but still, she didn't risk it.

Bella leaned against the shelves. At the end of the aisle, Lucas studied his list.

How was she not vetting women left and right to be in his mere presence? Even haggard from a day of work, hanging her plaque and whatever else he did, Lucas was breathtaking. Hair perfect and his... whoa!

Alicia had truly twisted her thoughts around. Why was she still thinking about Lucas' relationship status and... and... why was her mind wandering far too low on him? *Ridiculous, Bella.*

But it was true. The guy rarely went out of his way to get a date. And even when women fell all over him, he'd only dated a select few in a decade's worth of knowing him.

Bella, trying to echo the deep timbre of Lucas' voice and distract herself from ridiculous thoughts, said, "How fast can we hustle back and..."

And she couldn't help but giggle wildly when he wheeled around at her imitation of him.

"You coming?" He called. "Or are you going to buy out the cereal bars?"

The giggles faded, but that left Bella standing there, staring at Lucas and his falling smile for way too long.

"Spit it out," he said as he doubled back to her, taking her elbow. "Are you that tired?" During his pause, Lucas leaned in to brush the hair off her face and look into her eyes.

A flush crept up Bella's neck and cheeks. Lucas' clear blue eyes searched hers.

But a second later, he rustled her hair again, hand held out, waiting for her to fork over the basket. "I could have come alone. Do you want to wait in the car? This won't take me much longer."

They had seen no one else in the claustrophobically compact store, yet Bella felt a fiery heat rise through her throat.

"What?" She shook off the remnants of the daze she'd been in. "And miss out on another Lucas Holt heart attack?"

Lucas said, "Oh, thanks. Only had three today."

Her hand slipped into the crook of Lucas' arm. Comfortable and secure and...

Man, he would never find a girlfriend constantly hanging out with *the* social pariah of New York City. AKA Bella. He took her grocery shopping and fell asleep on her couch to old Christmas movies. Worse, he was probably clear as day in the tabloid pictures. She was ruining his social life by association. Here.

In Kalamazoo...

Oh God, Kalamazoo.

Bella had so many questions she'd never thought to ask before.

What the hell is going on for Christmas? Have you completely written me out of your Christmas plans after five years? Do you just want to video chat like every Christmas since I left, and you can go spend a peaceful Christmas with your family because you have better things to do and...

"Hey, Lucas?"

He stopped and took her basket, eyebrows knit tightly together. "Go sit in the car. I got this. I never should have..." Balancing the two baskets, Lucas dug for his keys in his pocket.

"No," she yanked it back again and choked out, "Christmas?"

"What about Christmas?"

This felt like the dumbest question ever. Especially with how much Lucas was worrying about her.

But the Holt Family Christmas? Tears welled in her eyes. Of all the things changing in her life, Bella could not bear the thought of losing what made Christmas special.

Lucas' holiday plans could have changed, and did she even ask?

Everything, every single thing in her life, kept changing without her input.

"Never mind," Bella said. *Dumb. Dumb, dumb, dumb.*

Yet Lucas knew and said, "We fly out on Christmas Eve. Like always."

Bella caught the tail end of a smile before he turned and continued shopping.

Like always?

Bella followed Lucas to the next aisle, though her knees wobbled. Lucas raided the pasta aisle for dry ingredients to go with the chicken and fresh veggies in his basket. Still, Bella's mind kept returning to the thought that Christmas would be normal, and relief overwhelmed her. Last year's Christmas wasn't typical, but it was the best Christmas in years. She'd been reunited with her brother and Lucas.

One year earlier

Bella

Bella felt groggy. She didn't remember anything like where she was or how she got there. Every muscle, every joint, every single part of her ached. Everywhere.

What happened?

Her eyelids were so heavy they resisted opening, but she could tell the room she was in was dark. And freezing.

The sheets covering her were thin. Bella had no desire to move. Her chest felt heavy like a weight sat there preventing her from moving. Pain shot through her shoulder when she tried turning her head. Far more pain than if she'd slept in a strange position. Something happened to her.

When she had the energy, Bella cracked her eyes open. Next to her was a silhouette, sleeping in a chair.

Her eyes fluttered closed again, exhausted.

Lucas' voice roused her again, though.

"I think she woke up." He was quiet, answering someone else in the shadows.

Soft grazes brushed her head, so she worked hard to open those insanely heavy lids again.

"Hey," Lucas whispered. "You're back."

"Where was I?"

He swallowed. Hovering at her head, glasses lopsided from sleeping in them. His blond hair was longer than she remembered and sticking every which way. She couldn't figure out how to lift her hand and fix everything. He wore a wrinkled suit like he'd come straight from work.

"Get more rest."

"Why're you here?" Her words slurred together. She was in... where was she again? They were in the... they were in...

"Merry Christmas, Bells."

Present Day

Bella

Back then, she never asked why Lucas was in Turkey with her for Christmas, helping her recover from her collarbone surgery after the explosion. He had a girlfriend and was set to go home for the Holt holiday celebrations.

Bella had Alicia. Plus, Chris dropped everything in his pathetically lonely life to fly over, which made sense, but Lucas had his own life.

She'd had a couple weeks between surgery and returning home to New York, which was short compared to the years Bella spent in Frontier Doctors. He could have waited to see her.

"Whatever happened to you and Nora?" The question was out before her rather holey internal filter stopped her. Of course, now she felt dizzy at what the potential answers could be.

Lucas

Rice. A good staple to have in Bella's pantry. There was a multitude of quick dishes he could cook with rice.

Lucas reached for the bag and froze at the question. Bella covered her mouth, swallowing a lump and smiling meekly.

"N-Nora?" Lucas asked.

The girl he was dating until about a year ago.

The girl who broke up with him when he ran to Bella's side after the explosion.

Really, that had been the final straw in their relationship, not the first.

She was *incredible,* intelligent, and stunning. Short wavy brown hair, athletic, and a grade school teacher. He met Nora jogging in Central Park.

"I just want to meet your family." Nora pleaded only days before the explosion. "You've taken your friends home. I'm your girlfriend. I-I..."

Lucas stopped her before the 'L' in love came out. No matter how incredible Nora was, he wasn't ready for the 'L' word.

He'd already hesitated several times to spend an entire night with her. And the few times they did... well...

Nora would ask about the t-shirt quilt and get upset Bella had made it. The pictures around the apartment were of his family, him, Bella, Chris, and Alicia traveling the United States. Bella even furnished his apartment with items from her own apartment because she was leaving for Frontier Doctors. Bella was across the world, but her mark was everywhere in Lucas' apartment.

Nora was most exasperated when, during one of the few nights she spent at Lucas' apartment, he woke up in the middle of the night to talk to Bella on video chat with Chris. She stormed out after the call ended, and he and Chris opted to start working earlier than usual. They laughed and planned what aid to send to Frontier Doctors from Astor Pharmaceuticals.

The last straw was when Lucas and Chris changed plans last minute. They dropped everything from work to packing to take a jet to Turkey, where Bella was transported for surgery. Literally, they told no one but Chris' assistant their destination, and when Nora found out, she was understandably pissed. Lucas said nothing to her, not even a text, which was solely on him. He'd gotten on the plane and collapsed into a fitful sleep.

It wasn't fair to Nora; he knew that.

After Bella had woken, Lucas was distracted learning about the care for Bella's injury and the planned rehab. Chris was fielding calls left and right, so neither Bella nor Lucas noticed when Chris took the call from Nora. The man said nothing about it until he'd dragged Lucas off to get coffee.

"Merry Christmas. You're single."

"What the fuck are you saying?"

The rare foul language from Lucas made Christian pause and grin.

"Nora called."

"Lucas?" Bella materialized in front of him, shaking his shoulder and jerking him back to the present.

He had to say something. Anything. But all that came out was a highly articulate, "Uh?" There was absolutely, positively no way he was telling Bella why Nora broke up with him.

Bella dropped a bag of rice into his basket, looping her arm through his. "You don't have to tell me."

His mouth was as dry as a desert. "W-why the sudden interest?" Words were slowly coming back to him.

She simply said, "Alicia's worried about you."

Bella

Alicia was worried and twisted Bella's mind into thinking about Lucas constantly. She needed to understand what happened, maybe so she could just move on.

"She was saying..."

Whoa! Bella caught the words before they escaped, literally slapping her mouth closed.

Lucas would laugh if she ever asked him to be her date. Maybe he'd be her pity date. The fallen socialite who can't get a man to stand next to her for a photo, let alone long enough to be her date anywhere.

They were both saved by the buzz. Lucas' phone jingled the keys in his pocket as texts came in hot and fast.

"Sounds important."

Bella untwisted herself from him.

The phone screen peeked out from his pocket for a second while he held down the power button.

"What're you doing?" Bella asked.

She glimpsed a girl's name, Melissa, before the shutdown screen came up. Her heart squeezed in her chest.

"It's not important," Lucas insisted.

"That many texts..."

Lucas held out his arm like a sleep-deprived knight in a not-so-shining, rumpled suit. "Just stuff for Santa's Village this weekend. We can worry about that later."

CHAPTER NINE
The Bet

Lucas

Lucas and Bella only had a few more items on the shopping list. During that time, Lucas couldn't help but replay those seconds between his phone blowing up and Bella's face. Did she see it? Did she believe him?

Melissa was nothing more than the woman who worked at Macy's, his contact for the upcoming Christmas giving tree event. She'd never texted outside of work hours, but the event was coming up that weekend, so of course, there would be last-minute logistics and details that needed to be hammered out, but that was a daytime concern. Not a 'now concern.'

Lucas led Bella to the front, his arm aching under the weight of the shopping basket.

A single, surly cashier manned the registers. Lucas wished they had more options. This woman, Zoe, always seemed to have shifts when he and Bella shopped and watched them wander the store with an unnerving hawk eye. He wasn't sure he'd ever seen her have a friendly smile, just a strained half grin when they entered the checkout lane.

Bella didn't notice. She was flipping through the latest issue of Business Insider. Her brother and his perfect toothy smile stared back at Lucas from the cover.

"Good evening," Zoe deadpanned. Sleek black hair, streaked with various colors, stuffed under a fluffy Santa hat. She wasn't much different in size than Bella, maybe a few inches taller, but her aura, if that was even the right word, was way more intimidating. Even in her green Food Emporium polo and mismatched Christmas swag.

Lucas couldn't seem to relax under Zoe's gaze. On the other hand, Bella was busy making popping noises and giggling at the article. And not paying attention to anything around her.

He yawned and stretched dramatically. Then sighed. Nothing from Bells other than a soft snort at the article she was reading. So, he pulled out his debit card and took the divider from between their groceries while Bella read on.

"Did you read Chris' interview? He talked about... Wait! What're you doing? Not fair!" Bella squealed, jumping at Lucas and reaching for his debit card. Zoe was already through most of Bella's groceries. "You. Paid. Last. Time!"

He squeezed his card, holding it in with the flat of his palm. His other hand free to bat Bells away and pray she didn't make him lose his grip and take the debit card.

"Then next time, pay attention!" He said and laughed.

Zoe was almost done scanning everything. He just had to keep his card in the reader while the last few items were scanned, and then the payment would go through. Bella rolled up the magazine and smacked him in the arm. She tossed it on the last of the groceries and glared. "This means war, Holt."

Well, that was a relief. War he could deal with. That was blessedly normal for Bella.

"What? Your investments make more in a month than I do in a year. But I do make enough to afford your groceries! Especially when you buy so little!"

Bella assaulted his arm. Bags piled at the end of the short lane to the point where Zoe cleared her throat several times, vying for their attention.

"Go warm up the car," Lucas said and tossed her his keys.

Bella loaded up her arms with as many bags as she could carry, staring daggers at him the entire time. Then, while backing her way out the exit, pointing from her eyes to his. "I'm watching you, Holt."

Lucas drank in the way Bella kept making faces at him as the payment processed.

The doors had barely closed when Zoe barked, "Okay. We got a bet!" And she sent Lucas into the neighboring cash register stand, panting.

He'd completely forgotten Zoe was there, observing them.

"Bet?" he asked, unsure and a little scared.

There were many times people asked Bells who she was or recognized her. Most notably, this happened during Alicia's non-bachelorette party. Alicia dragged everyone to a new club, the kind only the twins could get them into, to celebrate her last night single with her soon-to-be husband. The night was recorded for the world on Instagram by anyone at House of Yes.

So, was this a bet like who Bella was? Or...

Zoe held out the receipt for Lucas, then yanked it back out of reach when he tried to take it. "How long you been married?" she asked.

"M-married?"

What was going on?

"You got that cute thing going on still. Flirting and stuff. You're newlyweds, right?"

Somehow, as innocuous as the question was, Zoe was still utterly intimidating. Lucas lost his voice, trying to wrap his mind around the question.

"We're not...You're...well, that's not...no?" Lucas tried to settle on a single answer, but Zoe's expression intensified.

"Whole store," her hand circled around the store, "has a pot going. Because for months, we've been keeping tabs on your sickeningly cute flirting. And I want to win that pot. Give me the deets."

She reached across and grabbed his hand, then stuffed the receipt in.

"We're not m-married," he stuttered out.

Lucas tried to pull away, but she was strong.

"You're not what?"

"Together?" His voice cracked.

Wrong answer.

Zoe pulled him closer, her grip so strong Lucas tried to give her some slack before she popped his shoulder out of its socket. And he was strong. He could keep up with Bella on a mat when it came to boxing. For a few minutes at least. If she went easy on him.

"So, here's what I'm-a do. Because I know there's a few others here seeing me talk to you. I'm going to tell them all you cussed me the hell out, and I never found out anything new. By God, you are going to tell that damn girl what's going on up there in your ridiculously golden head!" She kept grumbling, "Six months we've been watching! Not even dating!"

The stress of Zoe's ranting made Lucas slip. "Been way longer than that." He said that out loud accidentally.

"Excuse me?" She whirled on him again.

"Oh, my God," Lucas said and snatched the remaining grocery bags and hustled out the door, hoping to save his ass.

Lucas crashed into the driver's seat with the rest of the bags in his lap while Bella fiddled with the radio. The bulk of those bags pushed the car horn, and he jumped again. Head crashing on the ceiling of the car.

"You okay?" Bella stopped on a Christmas radio station.

Lucas

Bella began nodding off only a few minutes into the show they'd chosen. Fifteen minutes was all she lasted after dinner. A full belly and slouching on the couch in hot debate zapped the last of her energy. Lucas arranged the comforter over her, and she threw half back on him.

From his peripheral vision, he caught her turn towards him, staring at him and not watching tv. Lucas had thrown the tie on the coffee table ages ago. He fiddled with the buttons on his wrists under her gaze.

"You won," he said *like always.*

"Thank you." Bella's hands, warm from the comforter, found his.

He wasn't sure what she was thanking him for. Dinner? The rescue? Groceries? It couldn't be anything else.

Bella threatened bodily harm if he finished doing the dishes because, as she said, "You've already done too much."

He tried to work it out. "You said thank you. Well, you said..."

"Not the dishes. I could still hire someone to do that stuff."

Laughable. The entire time he'd known Bella Astor, she rejected things like maids without outright leaving the family she loved dearly.

She squeezed his hand.

"I'll always be here, B."

Always.

No matter how dumb that was.

Christian

Chris' phone kept ringing, no matter how many times he pushed it to voicemail.

In the bed next to him, a woman moaned, "What's going on?"

"I have a call to take. Go back to sleep," Chris said simply, slipping out of the sheets.

Padding out into his kitchen in his slippers and boxers, Chris found his glasses next to the espresso machine. His glasses were rounder with a thick metal frame on top. Easy to tell the difference between his and Lucas' glasses, even when he was blind as a bat.

Alicia

37 missed calls.

His phone started vibrating again. Yet another incoming call from Alicia.

"What the fuck is so important?" Chris' voice bounced off the marble and white European-style cabinets. A soft glow illuminated the stainless steel appliances.

"Oh, did I interrupt your beauty sleep, you dumbass?" Alicia's voice was extra grating in the middle of the night.

"Yes. Yes, you did. Lovely to hear your dulcet tones at," he squinted at the clock on the oven, "three in the morning."

What could possibly be so important as to call at this time? On a weeknight.

"Have you not been online? Like at all?" Alicia was talking fast, almost hyper-caffeinated fast.

"Do you sleep?" Chris asked, raking his curls back.

"I asked first. And I woke up to pee."

"TMI, Alicia!"

"I can give you more details! Answer my question, Christian!"

"No," he said, fiddling with a handle on the espresso machine. "I was busy with..."

"A waitress?"

Close enough. Chris didn't feel the need to correct her. It was a restaurant manager who'd come to check on him.

Alicia growled, "Man! Pres showed up at the clinic after I left for the night! Every social has been blowing up since."

That had to have happened hours ago. Most nights, Bella was out after 7 PM.

But two nights of Preston encounters. Chris' imagination ran wild with what his sister could do.

"Shit. Shit...what do I...?" He started to panic, then stopped himself. Nothing too terrible could have happened. Neither Bella nor Lucas called. Most importantly, the police didn't call him.

"It's everywhere. Bella threw something at him. Someone across the street caught it on camera. You can see it through the blinds of the clinic windows, and then B comes out and yells at him. I can't get a hold of B or Lucas. Goes straight to voice-mail."

Another call beeped during Alicia's freak out. A detective Christian had enjoyed taking out for dinner. Someone he'd actually seen more than once.

"'Licia?" Chris begrudgingly pulled out the sweet tone, the cute nickname that Bella used when she begged Alicia for something. "Detective Sanders is calling."

But she was on a roll. "This isn't the time for a booty call! Or whatever..."

Well...

He hadn't been thinking of the detective lately, but now that he was, Chris started, "That..."

"Gross! Stop! Do *not* give me details!"

Chris added Detective Ami Sanders to the call. The picture on her contact profile was a pretty picture he'd taken on their third dinner out during the time his sister was overseas. A cute wavy bob, vibrant dark brown eyes, and glowing light brown skin. Very different than when Ami was working.

He turned his back on the bedroom, where — what was her name? — slept.

"Christian?" Ami said amidst breathing a sigh of relief.

"Ami? I'm a little booked this evening…" The last remnants of sleep were gone. He threw the girls on speaker and started pulling out coffee beans, his grinder, and more to make a latte.

Alicia snorted. In the background, clothes were rustling.

"Is the Bella Astor that owns Hope Clinic the same…"

"Jesus." Bending, Chris softly banged his head on the counter. "What the hell did she do?"

"Christian, can you confirm? Is the Bella Astor…"

"Yes, my sister owns Hope Clinic."

"Whoa! Co-owns! She owns half, you asshat!" Alicia interrupted.

There was a pause, and Chris swore he heard voices in the background. "Are you 'Dr. Alicia Mancini'?" Ami sounded like she was reading a report.

There was a simultaneous moan from both Chris and Alicia.

"I am. What did Bella do?"

"Dr. Astor was not involved. There's been an incident at the clinic. Her name and number were listed for contact, but we can't get a hold of Dr. Astor."

"Wait?" Abandoning the caffeine, Chris felt wildly awake. "Incident. What kind of incident?"

Detective Sanders hesitated. "Can you come down here? Both of you?"

CHAPTER TEN
Crumpled memories

Bella

Bella jerked awake. A loud crash above her or behind her or... well, it was loud. There were voices and...

"It's the neighbors upstairs," Lucas mumbled next to her. "Baby's awake."

Baby? Right, baby. Not...

Adrenaline pumped through her, her heart pounding. She was awake and there was no way she was going back to sleep.

Frontier Doctors made her a lighter sleeper than she'd ever been before.

"Hey," Lucas' voice was closer now. "It's okay. Nothing to worry about."

His voice was dreamy. Not... dreamy-dreamy, but... sleepy-dreamy. Bella controlled the panic racing through her. The thoughts she couldn't control about both Lucas and sudden noises.

"I know," Bella breathed, watching him push into the cushion, trying to get comfortable again. His hand blindly pawed for hers.

She knew there was nothing to worry about. She had to keep telling herself. Nothing was happening. Nothing urgent. Bella squeezed her eyes tight.

Seconds later, Lucas flipped on the lamp on the side table. On the cable box, the time shone. A little past 5 AM.

Bella tried not to look too shaken but still excused herself to the bathroom. Lucas didn't make a big deal about anything. No pity, and for that, she was eternally grateful.

At the door to the bathroom, she watched him lie on the couch for a moment, eyes fluttering again. He'd turned away from the lamp, trying to get more comfortable. Bella shut the bathroom door before turning on the light to not disturb Lucas further.

Sitting on the closed toilet seat, Bella's face fell into her hands. The heart palpitations slowed to an average, steady beat.

Another way she failed in life. Her dad never had these problems when he came back from Frontier Doctors. People — not just any people but her brother and mother — what would they think if they knew she had nightmares? What if Alicia knew? How was Lucas okay with her the way she was? Did he tell the others?

Stuffing her hands in her pockets, trying to get her mind off her failings, Bella rummaged around and found a crumpled piece of paper. Removing it, she unwadded the card, revealing a message.

You owe me for dry-cleaning. ~Pres

Asshole. Why did Bella even have it in her pocket? She tossed the card in the trash, not bothering to crush the message again. On the back was another scribble she hadn't seen before.

Need some help with my forward changes.

Huh.

When Pres and Bella entered high school, Pres joined Bella in ballroom dancing lessons. She'd started years before him, and Bella used to tutor him. Pres was surprisingly willing to learn the steps, especially if he didn't have to practice with their crotchety instructor, Mrs. Fenwick. That woman looked old enough to have invented ballroom dancing.

He used to write Bella notes to her like this when they were in high school. Not code, per se. The letters were filled with the names of ballroom dance moves, creating a message. He'd always write it on the back of a note from one of his friends. Somehow the wording sounded like it was intended for his guy buddies in case anyone ever intercepted the notes. The moves almost sounded like sports-related terms.

This time Bella picked up the note and crumpled it again before throwing it back in the garbage. That way, she wouldn't have to see Preston's perfect, prim, pompous handwriting any-more. When Bella looked at herself in the mirror, her face was a patchwork of red and pink, and a solitary wet streak ran the length of her cheek. She splashed cold water on her face, trying to hide the evidence. When she emerged from the bathroom, she prayed to every god she could think of that she looked nor-mal.

Lucas had neatly folded the comforter and now stood in the kitchen, staring at his phone. Bella crept towards him, hop-ing to startle Lucas with a playful pounce. Anything to take her mind off the horrible pit in her stomach. But when she got to the kitchen, Bella saw Lucas scrolling through last night's texts from Melissa.

All her desires evaporated. Bella forced herself to look away, her stomach roiling harder than ever.

"Bella?" Lucas asked.

She still stood frozen at the breakfast bar.

"Are you okay, Bells?"

"Yeah, no," Bella felt the lump in her throat grow. "I'm fine." She took a step back.

Then backed out of the kitchen. Bella kept her back to Lucas so he couldn't see her face.

"H-have you called her yet?" Bella forced the question out.

Lucas deserves to be happy. He should find someone that makes him happy.

And that thought shouldn't be hurting her.

"Who?" Lucas asked. The distinct rattle of the coffee pot coming out of the coffee maker, the water started running, echoed in the apartment.

"Melissa?"

Bella didn't have the energy to hop over the couch. Instead, she fell into the neatly arranged pillows, crushed the comforter, and grabbed the remote to turn on the news.

"For what?" Lucas answered, "Talked to her yesterday for the Santa's Village event."

Bella sat up. The volume on the TV was turned way down like *someone* was watching but wanted her to sleep. Closed captioning ran along the bottom of the screen, but she wasn't reading the captions.

Situated perfectly behind the reporter was Hope Clinic, lined with police tape. The cameraman's angle wasn't great, but Bella could tell something was written on the windows and door but not *what*.

What the hell was going on?

Where was her phone?

When she couldn't find her phone, Bella turned up the volume on the television. The clinic footage from overnight cut to a split screen of the reporter at the scene and some early morning anchors in the studio.

"One of two heirs to the Astor estate, Bella Astor has reemerged in the public eye after showing up a year ago in the Hamptons for rehab."

Half truth. She was in the Hamptons for a stupid plastic surgeon appointment her mother had made. All to have her scar along her collarbone 'fixed' and walked out about five seconds after meeting the asshole doctor.

"Infamously known for her sex tape when she was 17, and walking away from a major collision after drunk driving her Maserati weeks after—"

That was a complete load of crap she did not want to unpack.

"— and, many will remember her famous whirlwind romance with philanthropist, model and now, lawyer, Preston Warren Esquire."

"How can anyone forget what she did two days ago?"

"I feel like we're back in the early 2000s again. Bella Astor lives in the headlines."

"This isn't the same Bella Astor from a decade ago."

"Well, it is. But packing on a few more pounds."

"Only a few? I can't believe we're talking about the same girl."

Lucas snatched the remote out of her hand. He shut the TV off as a side-by-side comparison of Bella from college, her lithe, muscular dancer body. A picture from a few days ago, a closeup of what barely constituted love handles, came on the screen. Since college, Bella had maybe added ten pounds, probably mostly fat, because she barely had time to exercise anymore.

A cell phone, hers, dropped into her hand mid-boot cycle.

"Don't listen to them. It's..." Lucas' phone vibrated on the counter nonstop until he crossed the room and picked it up. "Whoa," he stared at the screen, free hand frozen halfway through his thick blond hair.

Bella watched him for a moment, then unlocked her own phone. Sixty missed calls and almost double that in texts.

She didn't have enough time to click on the messaging app before another call popped up on her screen.

Chris

Bella answered the call, curious and afraid that her brother was awake before her.

"Hello?" her brother asked, his relief palpable. "Holy shit, you picked up!"

"What is going on at my clinic?" Bella bit back another wave of tears.

"You need to come down here. Now."

CHAPTER ELEVEN
The aftermath (Again?)

Lucas

Trying to get Bella to think rationally about what was important was like trying to change the direction of a herd of rampaging children rushing a toy display with a carrot. He could dangle the sensible carrot all he wanted in front of her face, but she would not be diverted.

Lucas hoped she would calm down and shower because whatever happened was not so urgent that she couldn't take a few minutes to clean up. It would help. But the best he could do was convince her to take thirty seconds to change into clean clothes in exchange for one of her sugary cereal bars.

He had nothing else to change into, but that didn't matter. No cameras or reporters would be focused on him. The one thing Bella did wait long enough for was the coffee to finish brewing. Lucas filled two mugs with coffee, then steered Bella to his car.

Heading down to the street, Lucas caught Bella nose-diving into the digital abyss, reading all the texts she'd missed overnight. Then, when Lucas started his car and saw a flash of blue on her phone screen and knew she was logging into social media.

"No," Lucas said as he grappled one-handed for the phone while trying to turn into traffic.

"Just drive," Bella ordered.

"Bella! It's going to be nothing but nega..."

Her phone flew to the floor and bounced back into the glove box. Lucas grabbed her knee before her heel could come down on the phone.

This early in the morning, the streets of Astoria were still empty, so the drive to Hope Clinic was fast. Lucas turned onto 31st in a matter of minutes and found it packed with news vans, police cars, and lighting rigs, casting Hope Clinic in a bright wash.

Bella hopped out of the car before Lucas could shift into park.

Alicia and Chris stood at the edge of the circus, puffing out clouds of breath and dressed in jeans and thick winter jackets. They caught Bella as she attempted to careen right through the yellow police tape.

Lucas recognized a detective behind Chris, one that he was almost positive he'd seen more in dresses than the comfy pants suit she currently sported. She must have been on Christian's arm at a party.

Chris and Alicia said various versions of, "B! B! You need to calm down." Over and over.

"What the fuck happened to the clinic?"

As she introduced herself, Detective Sanders hustled a few more uniformed officers over to keep the media back. She took their small group inside through a sea of broken glass and spray-painted slurs on what was left of the door.

Lucas' breath hitched at the destruction in the clinic. Chair cushions were ripped apart. The windows were obliterated, and curses spray-painted inside and outside the clinic made Lucas' vision swim.

He missed out on the beginning of Detective Sander's explanation, coming in at, "Dr. Mancini has been providing us with the inventory you both keep on hand. It doesn't appear that anything was stolen. The refrigerators look untouched. It's just physical damage."

Physical? This was more like freaking psychological warfare.

Lucas stood in front of the watercolor paintings and plaque, trying to find the right words for how he felt. This was a tangible reminder of what some people thought of Bella. And then there was the front desk.

"Are there any security cameras?" Detective Sanders asked unabashedly.

Bella moved around the waiting room, zombie-like, taking in everything but not saying a word. Detective Sanders asked again, and Lucas answered, "Just in the back. Where they store the medicine."

"And you are?" The detective pulled out a notebook. Her badge gleamed in the light from the news truck's rigging.

Chris answered when no one else said anything. "Lucas is Director of Distribution at Astor Pharm. He had a hand in procuring this site for Bella and Alicia's clinic."

"I've seen you before..." Detective Sanders said and narrowed her eyes at him.

And Lucas now remembered making Chris breakfast one morning and Detective Sanders coming out of Chris' bathroom, wrapped in a towel. Then returning to the living room in a velvety-looking gown and damp hair. He'd probably seen her the night before, too, on Chris' arm. But seeing a woman in Chris' condo? That's why she stood out.

"I live..."

Chris coughed strategically, but it wasn't enough to cover the Detective's blush.

"...across the hall," Lucas finished.

"Right." Sanders hid a smile behind her notepad. "I remember. Omelet and coffee. It was a good omelet."

He tried to remember any other time he'd been in Chris' apartment when Chris had a woman over. Typically Chris preferred hiding out in Lucas' apartment, waiting for the woman of the night to leave.

"Crappy taste in coffee," Chris said.

Lucas considered firing back, but Bella stood stark still, staring at something on the desk. An officer watched over her, but she wasn't touching anything. She was just locked onto something on the desk.

Lucas went to her, paper and glass and plastic bits crunching underfoot, and whispered softly, "Let's get out of here. I doubt there's anything we can do." His fingers brushed her hand, and this time he took it in his palm and led her away.

"We've collected evidence. We'll be on scene for a little while longer to collect any surveillance footage from neighboring businesses."

Chris fidgeted with his hair, raking his hand through it every few seconds until he asked one last question. "When can we start the cleanup?"

Bella

Leave Preston Warren alone.

Every time Bella closed her eyes, she saw different phrases scrawled on the day planner on her desk or the words on the walls.

Whoever did it also started the hashtag trend on Twitter and Instagram, calling for Bella to be arrested for assault. Alicia said most people thought that was ridiculous. Only a few were using the hashtag seriously, but none of that changed how she felt.

This is the start.

She refused, flat out refused, to cry. Preston ate away at her soul, but this...she wouldn't let one news camera or cell phone video catch her crying.

Her brother and friends tried to shield Bella from the onslaught as they stepped out of Hope Clinic to regroup at Astor Pharm's offices, but Bella broke through her semi-circle of friends and walked straight to Lucas' car, head held high and straight. Ignoring every flash and question directed at her. She didn't slump in the seat while Lucas turned his car back towards Manhattan.

Somehow, for as chaotic as the street outside Hope Clinic was, Astor Pharm's headquarters was in an utter frenzy at a little past 6:30 in the morning. Security was in force, keeping people away from every entrance. Bella and Lucas waved into the executive garage with at least five guards keeping paparazzi at bay.

Lucas, already on edge from the last few days, hid in the corner of the executive elevator while they rode up to Chris' floor. He was more rumpled than ever with his shirt unbuttoned halfway down, his hair uncombed, and still wearing his glasses.

The elevator stopped at the executive floor. Lucas swiped his card across the reader to allow them access. Bella stepped out to the gray-toned steel and glass-decorated floor to an eerie silence. There was extra security, that was for sure. People on the phone, answering questions. But none too loudly. And all decidedly keeping to the elevator end of the floor.

Straight ahead was Chris' office, door wide open. Her brother and his mess of curls, merely a shadowy silhouette, stood stark still, staring out the window in his office at the early morning New York skyline.

Bella came up behind him and froze.

"Bella."

Her mother's voice turned Bella's blood to ice.

Alicia was nowhere in the office, but she must be in the building somewhere, just not in her mother's evil clutches.

Lucas stayed outside the doorway. She felt him there. Calm and resolute, and stole a glance at him through the door as he sighed and stuck his hands in his pockets. Lucas was obviously waiting like they all were for what was to come.

Her brother turned, tense and apologetic, and walked out of his office, closing the door behind him.

Lucas

"I can't believe you left her alone in there!" Lucas hissed. "She's your sister."

"He's still terrified of his mother," Alicia said, returning conveniently after Bella was locked in Chris' office in one-on-one combat with her mother.

Lucas had two words for Alicia. "Bridal. Shower."

Alicia grimaced but said nothing else.

The door was thick and soundproofed well, yet they all heard Lina Astor clear as day.

"The family name, Bella! For heaven's sake!"

Chris stood at his personal assistant's desk and held down the intercom button.

Bella's voice blared through the speaker. "What would you prefer, mother? Another sex tape?"

Chris let go of the button, but Alicia was right there to hit it again.

"Preston is the one..."

"Preston was civil! Extending the olive branch. You've act-ed like nothing more than..."

"I am pissed, mother! It may not have been the right thing to do, but does anyone ever stick up for me? Can you not blame me outright? I'm allowed to be angry with Preston for that whole shit show before I left! For being an ass. For never actu-ally helping! He just shows up and expects me to be *fine* with it all."

"This isn't Tyler Montefort and..."

Lucas removed Alicia's hand from the button. He had no idea what, if anything, Alicia knew about the sex-tape fiasco from Bella's senior year of high school. Besides what the media portrayed... which was less than accurate.

"What?" Chris asked when he caught Lucas analyzing him.

Chris avoided looking at the door or the intercom. His friend's hair was becoming oily from running his hands through it so much.

Then the hammer dropped. Coming straight through Chris' office door.

"The goddamn media said more about my weight than what happened to the clinic!"

Chris flipped the button on the intercom again to hear his mother coolly reply, "Astor's have an image to uphold. You could stand..."

That was the final straw. Chris flew through the door of his office.

CHAPTER TWELVE
The last few days have been nothing but bad ideas

Lucas

Chris crashed through the door, narrowly avoiding his sister as she stormed out, muttering, "I have an image for people..."

That image included her scratching her hairline with her middle finger, and Lucas' imagination supplied scenarios of what she might be planning next.

Security, managers, lawyers, and PR people who were congregated near the elevator cleared a path for the fuming heiress. Chris shot his mother a glare, but it withered almost instantly.

"Smooth," Alicia cooed at the younger Astor twin.

Based on the bags under Chris' eyes, he looked to be running on about as much sleep as Lucas. And his sense of humor was stretched thin.

"Bella! Bella Annalise Astor!" Lina shouted too late.

Bella was in the elevator, doors closing and possibly flipping her mother off.

"Christian?" Lina fiercely growled.

Chris rolled his eyes. "I will send a security detail after Bella, Mother."

"Security?" Lucas said and let out a sigh.

What better way to piss Bella off even more than she already was? Send a personal detail to crowd her. Even when they were invisible, they weren't invisible to her. Lucas easily forgot that they were there until a flick of Bella's eyes indicated where one was. Since she wasn't in the public eye, most of her day-to-day required little security, but those days were probably ending after recent events.

He bit back what he wanted to say, opting for, "Chris? No, Bells will..."

Chris wasn't listening. He wandered away from his office, already on the phone with Bella's personal head of security, Kellan Travers.

"This is a bad idea," Alicia sang.

Lucas wholeheartedly agreed.

When Chris returned, Lucas asked, "How is Kellan?"

Since Bella's triumphant return to New York, she'd gotten a new head of security. The man looked like he'd come straight out of the army. Actually, Kellan and Bella were about the same age. Kellan, though, was taller than Lucas and built more like an Armani-wrapped tank.

Chris beamed. "Kellan is heading to Bella's gym."

"Great! I'm not going anywhere near her!" Alicia announced.

No one, especially Lucas, blamed Alicia for that sentiment. Bella's preferred method of letting out her aggression was punching things. Usually people. But with purpose. She liked to box and took jiu-jitsu at one point. She was vicious on the mat. He'd often trailed her to the gym and sparred with her to let out the pent-up aggression after arguments with her mother. Usually, that led to days of Lucas poorly hiding the fact that he needed to ice his shoulders. Bella had a mean right hook and jab. And cross. And her submissions...

Lucas' mind stopped. Bella didn't have time for the gym lately.

Chris beamed.

Alicia shrugged, balled hands on her waist, waiting impatiently for an answer.

"Bella hasn't been to the gym since she came home. Not her normal gym, at least." Chris whispered.

Okay, information such as that was a double-edged sword. Chris wasn't pissing his sister off more by crowding her. Which was good. But he was keeping close tabs on what she was doing, which... was kind of awkward to be in the middle of.

"So?" Alicia shrank as morning light hit Christian and Lucas.

Lina Astor stood at the door of her son's office, shooting icy daggers at them all. As if she blamed them for not stopping Bella from being Bella. Lucas could hear the accusations play through his mind now.

"I volunteer as tribute to talk to Bella," Alicia said.

"Weren't you just making fun of Chris for being scared of his mom?" Lucas asked under his breath. "Are you scared of... Mrs. Astor?" He gulped.

Point of fact, Lucas was not only still terrified of his own mother but even more terrified of both Lina Astor and Alicia's mom. He may have only met Alicia's mom at Alicia's wedding, but it was enough.

"It's still like dibs. I'll talk to B. You boys can..." She motioned at Mrs. Astor in the doorway.

Lina Astor methodically rapped each perfectly painted nail against the metal door frame. Alicia couldn't form another word. She bowed out, hustling for the elevator without another glance back at the boys or Lina Astor.

And that left Chris and Lucas to deal with the ice queen.

Bella

Although, until this point it had been a bright, icy morning, the sun currently hid behind clouds, casting more shadows than the plywood coverings over the windows. There should be light and hope in this small building. It's where they had gotten the name. Hope Clinic.

Bella stood in the doorway for a long while, staring at the destruction of all the good she'd built.

Her brother probably had a plan for cleaning up the clinic. Chris enjoyed making plans. He'd hire people to clean up the physical mess, thin and remove the paint sprayed on the walls and desk.

Going further than the first step past the police tape, Bella took a shaky breath. Where could *she* start? She wanted to clean everything all at once.

The simple answer was sweeping the floor. Bella felt like she was on autopilot, wading through debris to grab the broom and dustpan from the back storage room. Bella began sweeping up the bits of glass, plastic, and whatever else had been smashed in the waiting room. She moved slowly, lost in every mistake she'd made over the last couple of days. Despite popular belief, Bella was capable of restraining herself. She generally did well not pummeling paparazzi with their own cameras.

Preston, though, always pressed the proper sequence of buttons to set her off.

At some point, Alicia showed up, watching from the doorway. Bella noticed her and waited, letting her friend make the first move.

"I'm sorry," Alicia said while Bella was mid-broom stroke.

"Why are you apologizing?" Bella asked, leaning on her broom. "Were you getting a late-night caffeine fix and posted the video?" Those words came out harsher than she'd meant them.

Even without makeup, Alicia and her natural beauty left Bella a tiny bit jealous. She could imagine the newscasters stuck on Bella's appearance early that morning, mocking how she looked now. Hell, between the subway station and clinic, she'd seen the morning edition of the tabloid. Grainy pictures of Bella plastered across the front page, mid-rant pulled straight from the cell phone video. The worst possible quality video at the worst possible time was what Bella Astor would always be remembered for. And each page was filled with biting comments based on her lowest low.

She was sure there wasn't a single kind comment made in any media about her since she'd come home. Instead, it was attack after attack on her physical appearance, fights with Preston, and mistakes.

Now, though? Bella hid in plain sight. Hair tossed up in a messy bun and sunglasses kept more New Yorkers at bay than she'd thought. No one recognized her as the girl in the news or on the tabloids. She made herself not really look like whatever the hell she was now. Socialite. Starlet. Heiress.

Screw up.

Alicia looked more the part of an infamous socialite than Bella did.

"Fuck no," Alicia said. "But someone knows how to make me feel like shit..."

With a smirk, Bella said, "Chris' intercom isn't as silent as he thinks. I know you heard everything."

Alicia bent, helping Bella sweep the broken bits of her life into the dustpan. "Not... everything."

Bella expected suits or plain clothes security sweeping the street, vetting everyone, including the freaking coffee shop employees or standing guard around both women.

"Where's Kellan and the team?"

Alicia's smile faded. "Chris sent them to the gym."

A wild goose chase. That was surprisingly sweet.

Bella returned to sweeping, though there was almost no debris left this far in the corner.

"I'm sorry, B. I was thinking a lot about the last couple of days on the drive back." Alicia's voice cracked. "We *are* on your side. You know that, right?" But she couldn't quite bring her eyes to meet Bella's. "And you're right."

"About?"

"We shouldn't jump to conclusions. That whatever happens is your fault." Alicia slid next to her. "Bella, you have every right to be angry with Preston."

Just hearing those words, Bella exhaled a breath she'd been holding.

"But..." Alicia started.

Oh, wonderful. It was too good to be true.

Bella snapped, "But what? I wasn't fair to Preston? I should hear Pres out? It was Chris'..."

"Fiancé. Bella, I remember." Alicia grabbed the broom and set it to the side when Bella relented. "But..."

"Pres knew exactly how I felt going into our relationship." Bella snatched the broom back and found another spot full of broken glass. "*I* knew better than anyone what he was like before. I watched the trail he left behind. How Chris tried to keep up with Pres. Pres *promised me* he would never do that to me. That I wasn't those other girls, Alicia. That I was different. That together we'd be different. Not like our *friends* from school. Not like his father, who had mistress after mistress, and his mother just took it and never said one word. The least he could fucking do was own up for all that back then and all this now. But he can't. It's jokes and charm, and he just wants me to forget it ever happened. Go back to how things were before."

Moving into Bella's path, Alicia tried to keep Bella's eyes on hers. "I remember the conversations and the late nights talking about the pros and cons of dating that handsome POS. Look, B, yesterday... those jokes about Preston and what a guy needs to do... You know that all those thoughts are superficial. What's important is that... I just want you to be happy. The jokes weren't the best idea, *but* I think you need some closure with Pres. I think it would help. I'm not saying to open back up to him. But maybe talk to him? Find actual closure. You both still move in the same circles. He unfathomably still works for your brother. You'll inevitably run into him from time to time."

Bella thought that throwing the contents of her bookcases constituted a pretty firm ending to the relationship.

But... Alicia made a point. More than one.

"And B? You talk to Lucas about everything, but you can talk to me. I'm always in your corner."

Bella gave a choked half sob, half laugh, and threw herself into Alicia for a hug when Kellan cleared his throat in the doorway.

"Busted." Alicia sighed.

"Mrs. Mancini, I know Ms. Astor well enough to not bring the whole crew. She'd just slip out again. Or punch them. But it is my job to keep Bella safe." Kellan tossed his sunglasses in his pocket, "I'm going to get coffee. For a while."

Alicia eyed Kellan longingly until Bella nudged her. "What? B, he wants to keep you safe..."

"Oh, my God."

"You surround yourself with a lot of hot men."

"I'm going to clean."

Cleaning felt never ending. They swept, and Bella talked more with Alicia than she had in months. Things she didn't tell anyone, even Lucas (though that man was kind of a mind reader and didn't need Bella to say the words to understand).

Inside their tiny, broken clinic, the outside world was blocked out. Finally, when Bella couldn't sweep any longer, she collapsed into a waiting room chair while Alicia tugged on her to keep moving. They were both physically and mentally exhausted, but the clinic looked like their clinic again.

Neither kept track of how much time passed cleaning. A sudden knock on the door startled them both. As Bella answered the door, Alicia clutched the cleaning spray and rag like a weapon.

On the sidewalk stood Ms. Langry, a young single mom, her young daughter, Emma, clutching her. Running to a hospital wasn't an option.

"I saw the news but didn't know what else to do. Emma's fever got worse, and the phones..." Ms. Langry only paused for a breath when Bella placed a hand on the woman's full hands.

Bella grappled for the woman's first name. It was on the tip of her tongue. "Avery," Bella said triumphantly. "No, of course. Come in. I mean... It's a mess, but we can..."

Up the street, shouts rang and moved closer. Instinct pushed Bella into Ms. Langry, hugging them close, her back facing the street. Something exploded across Bella's side and back. Covering Bella in a multitude of fluids and smells.

"Shit!" she screeched.

As Alicia later confirmed, yes, there was actual shit on her.

"Assholes! What the hell?" Alicia tried snapping pictures of the car, but it was out of range so fast she only got the color and type.

Bella roared. Her ears pounded. She felt tugs and knew people were talking and pulling on her, but she shook them off and was moving down the street and descending stairs with no other thought than ending this torture. Now.

Alicia

Yelling didn't get through to Bella. And Alicia couldn't follow, not with a sick patient waiting.

Kellan ran across the street, apologies spewing out. Too late to do anything else but make sure Ms. Langry was okay. They assured Kellan they were all fine, which Kellan did not believe for a second. Alicia mentioned he might want to get his team to find Bella. Kellan already had a good idea of where to start.

Alicia whipped out her phone and typed: *I swear. I didn't mean for B to get arrested today. But you might want to have bail money ready.*

Chris' response was immediate. *Where is she going?*

Alicia: *Probably wherever Preston is at this moment? And Kellan is here. He's sending security out.*

As a final thought, Alicia added: *Call the lawyers. Just in case.*

CHAPTER THIRTEEN
One pungent lunch date

Lucas

Locks of damp blond hair clung to Lucas' neck. He felt a new tickle as some pieces brushed his cheek. Lucas removed the baseball cap, keeping most of the mess at bay, combed back as much as he could with his fingers, and replaced the cap backward this time.

There were a bunch of meetings soon to update him on issues with a shipping container stuck in customs in the United Kingdom and another entering Asia. He didn't want to leave for Christmas with these issues still in limbo. He sat at his massive desk, which was far too big for his office, but Chris insisted on gifting him the damn thing. Lucas pulled up the newest reports and emails to review for his first meeting. Next to his monitor was a framed picture of the twins and Lucas in front of his parent's Christmas tree from nearly six years ago. Bella and Lucas in matching ugly sweaters lit with battery-operated mini-light strings zigzagging across gold-trimmed Christmas trees. Chris refused to be sandwiched between them and their hideous sweaters. In fact, Chris even stood away from his sister by a whole foot.

"Holy crap! What the hell is that?" Chris gasped at Lucas from the door of Lucas' office like he was wearing that ugly sweater again. Clearly, he'd escaped his mother's clutches and come to torture him right when Lucas finally found his work rhythm.

"What? Want to send me home for breaking the dress code?" Lucas glanced at his plain white t-shirt, gym shorts, and sneakers. "This was the only thing I had in my gym locker. Because apparently Daniel doesn't only do his job. I would think the Finance Director has more to do than steal my suit to have cleaned."

"I hope he had it burned."

Lucas pushed up his glasses with his middle finger, a sign he had spent too much time with Bella. "I have a job to do. Don't you? Surely there is more to do than deal with your mother's obsession with PR."

"My mother has a point. Bella's PR can affect the business." Chris sighed. "Also, I have plenty on my plate."

Sure you do, Lucas thought.

"The Foundation my father built..."

"I don't have time for a novel. There's a meeting coming up in twenty minutes. What do you need?" Lucas glanced at the calendar on his computer monitor, double-checking his schedule.

"You don't have a meeting. We're having lunch." The further Chris slouched in Lucas' guest seat, the more he looked like a child. It mirrored how Lucas felt laughably out-of-place even after seven years working at Astor Pharm full time and years' worth of internships with Eli Astor. Like he was an imposter playing dress-up.

"I literally have a meeting in..." Lucas hit refresh, and the meeting disappeared from his calendar.

"Daniel cleared the next couple of hours." Usually, Chris would give him a Cheshire grin, but not today.

"I... hate you."

Daniel seriously did both his old job as a personal assistant and his new job co-currently. He could not leave these little jobs like anticipating an Astor's request to the new assistants.

"I need your help." He fiddled with the top button of his blazer. "Truly. I need you to..."

"No," Lucas said.

"...have lunch..."

"Absolutely not," Lucas interrupted again.

"With Preston and I."

Lucas took a moment before answering, sizing up Chris sitting calmly in his guest seat. Years of friendship meant Lucas knew when Chris was plotting, but not what he was plotting. The first question he could think of was, "Will Bella be there?"

"Of course not."

Immediately, Lucas' next question was, "What part of that idiotic plan did you think was a good idea?" Lucas threw down the pencil he'd been fidgeting with. "Huh? If she's not there, I'll punch that goatee right off..."

"You really spend too much time with Bella," Chris said, and finally, his Cheshire grin broke out.

"I'm not..."

One phone, Chris', buzzed with an incoming text. Then another text followed by Lucas' phone buzzing. Texts from Alicia came streaming in.

Certain words stuck in Lucas' mind from Alicia's texts.

Bella. Arrested. Bail money. Preston. Lawyer.

Lucas wrenched open the top drawer of his desk. "I guess I'm going to lunch with you." Lucas pulled out a set of car keys from the drawer and two bags of peanut butter M&M's.

"What's that?"

"Bella's favorite."

"No! That's... no!" Chris swatted at Lucas' hand, trying to snatch the bags of M&M's right out of his hand. "She loves that chocolate from Germany my father always brought home."

"Bella loves peanut butter. Specifically, peanut butter M&M's." Lucas dropped the bags in his shorts pocket. "She can love both."

Plus, watching Bella attack Preston required snacks. Hence, he needed a bag for himself.

"Gross," Chris grimaced.

Bella

Lunch in New York, particularly a lunch of a certain status, only happened at a handful of restaurants. Most high-end restaurants opened only for dinner, so few restaurants were open and up to Preston Warren's standards. A restaurant close to his office narrowed the field even more.

She had no cell phone signal in the subway, but Bella had a pretty good idea of where to head. The 7th Avenue stop would be closest to the Warren offices and within walking distance of several Michelin restaurants.

Sitting in the subway car, Bella lost the sense of whatever she was covered in, but the people around her were pinching their noses. And actually staring. Not blatantly ignoring her, as per New York tradition.

Bella felt like eyes followed her progress everywhere. Out of the subway car at 7th, up the stairs, and toward the Warren office.

Standing on the corner, Bella did the calculations. Pres enjoyed a view, and she knew there were many that he enjoyed regularly. Man wants a view and obscenely expensive dining before noon near his office? Bella headed straight to The Modern. In only a couple minutes, she saw the bright floor-to-ceiling wall of windows with patrons in the midst of being seated at a window near the door gawking at her. During the day, the restaurant was awash in whites and light everywhere.

Bella slammed through the front door and spotted Preston in the middle of the window seating, reading the menu. As far as she could tell, he didn't see her coming up the street.

At once, a hostess, maître d', and a manager all approached Bella and her literally shit-stained clothes. She wheeled on them at the first discreet, "Excuse me," one of them dared to say to her.

"Don't tell me to leave! I'm a goddamn Astor! And I need to speak to that asshole."

The word Astor caused them to back off. Bella hated invoking her surname but right now appreciated the power it held.

The Modern was not packed to the brim with patrons for an early Thursday lunch. But the patrons there fixated on 'Bella-hot-mess Astor' stomping through the restaurant. Including Preston.

Pres pressed a hand along his hair, not through it since that would muss it all up. As if that would ever matter. Nine times out of ten, Pres' hair bounced back to its perfect coif. Pres wore one of his immaculately tailored navy blue Burberry suits, which accented his broad chest. Fists clenched tight, Bella fought to not grab the first free item and lob it at his face.

She stormed to him, shoving Preston back into his seat when he tried to stand and offer her a chair.

"Bella?" He reached out for her hand, and she jerked it away. "Let's go somewhere..."

"Private?" Bella left delusions of being quiet behind at the clinic. "No! I'm not going somewhere fucking quiet, Preston! People are going to put this up on the internet, then so fucking be it! I was the villain before, and I will be the villain again. I am always the goddamn villain in this story! But I am done! People have been attacking me since I could walk! But you? You're the prince of this city! You never ever have to take responsibility for your actions, but Preston, they have real-world consequences! And I don't care! I don't! Let me be the villain, but your inaction, not speaking out about these videos and news stories, is getting other people hurt! Not 'maybe,' but is! My patients! Mine! Can't come into my clinic without being attacked!" She'd run out of steam. Preston sat in the chair, letting her rant, and he looked... surprisingly apologetic. Like he actually had some kind of *feelings* over what happened.

"Are you...?"

"Don't you dare! Don't!" All the energy Bella had been storing waned. "You're a Warren. You have the power to fix this. That's all I'm asking. For once, own up to your mistakes. Explain to the world that I'm not some bad guy that needs to be attacked so my patients can come and see me. Safely."

On the table, Preston's phone sat in an empty water glass. He reached to grab it first, but Bella was faster.

Pres shrugged, "We're live."

"We're WHAT?"

She saw he was logged into his social media and streaming live. The video had been pointed right at Bella. Now it showed her feet and Pres' moving into the frame. He'd stood and was right next to her.

His hands, warm and soft, cupped hers, fingers trying to open her palms.

"You're right. I didn't do anything to protect you, Bella. I was an asshole, and I should have done so much more, and I'm sorry. What those people did to your clinic disgusts me. I never thought that something like that would ever happen. Bella, I'm sorry."

She glanced down at the screen. Comments scrolled past, asking if this was real or staged and what the hell was happening. Bella ended the live stream. She threw the phone back on the table and jerked herself back.

At least one person within the restaurant had to have been live or recording, too. There was no way not one employee or patron wasn't filming. The social media story would keep going.

"Bella-donna," Pres whispered, and she pulled another step away from Pres at the nickname, trying not to think about the hundreds of times he'd whispered it in her ear. "You've always been right. I never stood up for you."

Her mind was empty. Like a void was left in her brain's place.

"Can we talk?" Pres circled the table to pull out a chair for her. He also motioned to the young brunette hostess, waving the woman away.

"There's no silverware on the table," Bella noted coldly.

He knew she was coming and had expected silverware, or almost anything, on the table would be a poor idea to have in arm's reach of Bella. New rage burned in her chest.

"Yes." Pres drummed the chair he held for her. "I saw the anonymous video. Do you...?"

He moved to take off his suit jacket, and she slapped him, growling, "No."

"I'm sure you have questions, Bella. Where do you want to start?"

Did she have questions? She was drowning in questions, and this might be the only time she was calm enough to ask them.

The only question she latched onto was, "Why... were you at the gallery?"

Pres gripped the back of the chair, his knuckles a bright white, and chuckled. Around them, people were still gawking, but it was the phones pointed at them that Pres withered under. "Can we please move this conversation to a more private location?"

Bella stood resolute, arms folded over the stains, food, and whatever else was stuck to her.

"I went to the opening of the exhibit. Evan, the photojournalist you met in Syria, is a friend of my father's. I've known him for years. And I saw you there. In the photos." Pres stood up, opening himself up for people to see him. Get the best angle. "And Lina was at the opening."

She let a groan escape at that. "Oh, my God."

"Lina said you were getting an award. I just wanted to congratulate you. And I thought... well... I wanted to see how you were after what happened."

She muttered, punctuating the last few words with a punch of the table, "The explosion. There was an explosion. A bomb. Just say the damn words."

"I was relieved. You look..." He stopped and started again, "I made a lot of mistakes."

"Is that code for you slept with a lot of women?"

"No. I never slept with other women when we were dating. That night, before you left, was..."

Bella thought Pres was going to say accident but thought better of it. Definitely the right call.

"I had your grandmother's ring. But you were leaving."

"I'd talked about that trip for years. It wasn't *news,* Pres! You knew I was leaving but that I was coming back. "

"I know. But you were going and didn't know how long you would be gone. You were gone four years. And almost didn't even come back to us."

"I don't owe you an explanation now for how long I was gone when we weren't together."

And it wasn't a secret with Lucas, Chris, or Alicia that she'd stayed longer because part of her couldn't face Pres again. Not yet.

He continued, "You're right. You're always right, Bella. I should have stepped up a long time ago. Even before we dated."

A waiter appeared with two glasses of water and a tray of assorted appetizers, sweating profusely.

"Do you want to stay? Join me for lunch?" Pres leaned forward, reaching out for her hand. "We could catch up?"

"No," Another step back. "I don't want to stay."

Murmurs spread through the restaurant-goers as a paper ripped. The tearing sound was as loud as a scream.

Bella swung around to see Lucas standing in the middle of the restaurant, ripping open a package of M&M's. He had damp hair and was in his gym clothes. Not even a jacket in the middle of winter. Chris sidled away from him but also waved away the approaching maître d'. Preston appeared next to Bella, jacket off this time.

"Want me to drive you home?" Pres asked. "We could finish..."

Bella swung back. "No."

Pres wrinkled his nose at her, a stark reminder that she was still covered in garbage that would ruin his jacket.

"But maybe, one day, you can tell me what the fuck happened the night before I left. But, for today, I'm done." Pulling away, Bella said, "Goodbye, Pres."

A smile tugged at her cheeks.

"See you around, Bella-donna."

She shook her head at him. "I'm not that anymore. Not to you."

"Understood." And Pres bowed to her.

Bella crossed the restaurant to her brother and Lucas, holding a hand demanding a palmful of candy. Lucas held one candy over her head and dropped it when she opened her mouth.

"That's unbearable," Chris said.

Her hand held out, Bella pleaded for a handful, and Chris snatched her wrist as he abruptly let go and asked, "What are you covered in?"

"What does it look like?" Bella quipped.

"That's disgusting," Chris shuddered.

Despite the garbage, Lucas slipped an arm around Bella, pulling her into a hug. Playfully, he ruffled her hair and slipped his hat off and onto her head. He looked past Bella and gave Pres a terse wave.

"Come on, the valet wouldn't park Lucas' piece of crap car." Chris pinched his nose closed. "And I'm so grateful I called for a separate car. You can go with Lucas since not*hing else* can ruin that piece of crap."

Lucas rolled his eyes and said, "You look better."

"I feel better." And she wasn't just saying she was better.

For the first time in a long, long time, she felt free.

CHAPTER FOURTEEN
Did someone break in?

Bella

Bella took the rest of the day off. Not because her brother insisted vehemently that she should go home. Also, not because Alicia messaged that the contractors arrived and were in the process of cleaning and replacing windows.

She took the rest of the day off because she needed to.

Lucas drove her home with the heat blasting since they were both jacket-less. Finally, after *everything*, Bella stood in her living room, alone, and fully appreciated how much she smelled of hot garbage. So, she luxuriated in a long, hot shower.

Patting her hair dry, Bella paced her apartment. Rarely did she stop or have a day off, even on the weekends. Now Bella had enough time to pause and think. Somehow, it was already less than two weeks before Christmas, and she only now realized that there wasn't a single Christmas decoration in her entire apartment.

With such a tiny apartment, Bella didn't have room to store all her belongings. Some of what she owned before Frontier Doctors furnished Lucas' condo. What she left behind sat in boxes in the condo next to Chris'. The one he'd bought for her. When she moved home, Bella took what she needed and left the rest in the unoccupied condo. Of course, Bella didn't need her Christmas decorations when she moved in.

Now? The small long space of her apartment felt empty and cold without lights, garland, and a tree. Bella had the sudden urge to fill every open space she could and add cheer to her gloomy few rooms.

Before she knew it, Bella was back in the subway and uptown. She resolved to call Chris' driver before he left work... both to help get her Christmas decorations back to her apartment and to piss Christian off that she'd stolen him. Just for fun.

Bella had the codes and keys to get on the Astor floor of The Century. Harold, the sweet older doorman with thick, Clooney-esque hair, pulled the door open and gave Bella a bow.

"Harold, grandkids still kicking ass in theatre?" Bella asked after hopping through the held open doorway.

"Charlie was Jo-Jo, and Kelsey was the snobby little girl. Charlie had me weeping the entire time."

Aw. Bella's lip quivered. They'd been in the play 'A home for Jo-Jo.' Her mind played images of the kids she'd seen in pictures up on stage in cute costumes.

"Did you send the kids to..."

"... Jordan?" Harold paused, realizing he shouldn't cut a woman like an Astor off, but Bella waved the thought away. "Yes, ma'am."

"Don't 'ma'am' me!" Bella hissed through a grin.

She'd been friends with Jordan longer than Lucas and Alicia, but not by much. In high school, Jordan has been her dance partner in ballet. They'd done countless performances together, to the point he tried to convince her that they could make a career of it. But Bella wouldn't be swayed from her dream.

Harold continued, "Charlie's taken to ballet like a duck to water." The doorman pulled out his phone and showed Bella a video of Charlie, the only other boy in class with Jordan. A small girl danced with Charlie, practicing a dance Jordan and Bella knew well. From Prokofiev's Cinderella.

Bella hated pulling herself away, but she needed to get upstairs before getting wrapped up for hours in Harold's stories. She waved at Madeline at the front desk, smashed the elevator button, and waited less than a minute for the elevator. Inside, she swiped the keycard for the Astor's secure floor and entered the current passcode.

The ride up was short and lonely, which didn't help how this building always felt like their building alone. Rarely did she see others since their floor was private.

Bella's sneakers squeaked on the marble tile floor between the runner and the door to what should be her condo. On sparse occasions, Bella watched movies at Lucas' place, reveling in her old couch. Lucas tried to make her take it back when she came home.

Unlocking the door, Bella crept inside a condo that was practically identical to Chris', except that all the new furniture was covered in dust cloths. New York's lit skyline shone through the windows on the far wall. Twinkling and pretty as she stood above all those other buildings. She sighed and headed for the bedroom.

Hidden in the back closet of the bedroom, Bella found her boxes of Christmas decorations. They were hidden behind Chris' random clothes, old decor, and more he didn't want taking up space in his closets. She sat on the floor, legs crossed, checking which box contained what. In the third box, Bella came across her Christmas ornaments. Unlike her mother's hundreds of plain glittery baubles that decorated the Astor Christmas trees every year, Bella's ornaments were a hodge-podge she'd collected over the years. Handmade ornaments from vacation spots around the world, packed in their own smaller padded boxes. Also, ornaments Bella made with Lucas and his little sister Lexi every year in Michigan.

It was like looking back in a time capsule. Obviously, the last five years were missing. But aside from the last several years, there were yearly pictures of Lucas and the twins, Alicia and Bella, just the twins and Lucas and Bella. They'd framed all the images in popsicle sticks and painted them the entire spectrum of the rainbow.

Bella held a few ornaments, remembering the first time Lucas invited the twins back home with him. He'd put his foot down that it was dumb for the twins to go back to New York and spend the holidays alone in their mansion when their parents were headed to Europe.

Lucas used pictures of him and the twins with their fishing score of the year in a few picture ornaments. Chris' scowl elicited a giggle. He only went fishing because Bella wanted to go. Yet, every year, without fail, he was up before dawn, helping load the Holt's SUV, without complaint, and went fishing with them, grimacing in every picture Bella took.

Lucas

"Did you convince Daniel to have my car cleaned?" The question finally popped out while Lucas rode the elevator with Chris to their floor.

"She was covered in crap. Actual crap. Of course, I did."

Lucas noticed his car smelled fresh, as close to the 'new car' interior smell as a decade-old car could get, as soon as he opened the door.

"You didn't have to come back to work," Chris said. "You could have taken the rest of the day." Chris ruffled his floppy curls around.

Sure, deprive Chris of the right to annoy the hell out of him the entire drive back from the office. It was Chris' favorite pastime when he didn't have a date. Somehow, the guy constantly stooped to riding home with Chris. A freaking CEO, and he was carpooling in Lucas' crappy Corolla half the week.

"Why?" Lucas countered instead with, "Trauma from hugging your crap-covered sister or the trauma from seeing Preston Warren... yet again?"

"I was thinking the first one."

"I changed my shirt. Unlike you, I am not traumatized by the ordeal."

If anything, he had renewed hope. Lucas couldn't remember the last time Bella looked honestly... happy.

The elevator opened to their private floor, and both boys abruptly stopped. Light spilled out from the open condo door next to Chris' condo. And then a crash reverberated up the hallway.

No one had access to their floor. Security was airtight in this building. Chris' head of security changed the passcode weekly.

Another crash!

Lucas quietly padded to his door and checked the handle. It was locked. Chris did the same. The door for the fourth condo, the one next to Lucas', was closed. Only the one next to Chris' condo was open.

Silent protests from Chris didn't stop Lucas' advances. Chris pressed his phone to his ear and slapped Lucas' shoulder.

Fists raised to protect his face — from what, Lucas had no idea — Lucas hopped into the doorway.

Bella, in a clean sweater and jeans, her winter jacket on but unzipped, yelped and dropped a box of ornaments right near the threshold.

"What the hell are you doing here?" Chris squealed. Quickly, he turned around and told, presumably, the security office that there was no emergency.

"Picking up stuff that is *mine*. I still have a key, you know."

Lucas kneeled, flipped open the top of the box, and saw himself staring back. Pictures of Bella and Chris and him from over the last dozen years.

"Shit." Chris pocketed his phone, took his keys out, and started flipping them around his finger. "You could have called ahead."

"Once again, I have a key. I own this floor with you. Name is literally on the title."

Bella kneeled with Lucas. Fresh curls and the light scent of her perfume wafted to him. She looked more like Bella from before she'd gone into Frontier Doctors.

Her eyes met his, expectant and hopeful, and she asked, "Want to go get a Christmas tree tonight?"

"Huh?" Lucas was taken entirely off guard.

A glance at Chris didn't help. Damn it! That stupid Cheshire grin crept across Chris' face as he disappeared down the hall to his condo without another word.

Lucas turned back. Bella held the ornament that had been staring back at him a moment before. Their third Christmas together. A wistful smile crossed Bella's face.

"Christmas tree?" Lucas asked. "I'm sure we can find one somewhere."

Bella refused to leave the floor until she ensured any ornaments along the bottom of the box were safe after their fall. They both dove into the box, Lucas brushing Bella's hand with his. After all this time, how did those little touches still make his heart skip a beat or three?

Lucas' brain slugged along, reconciling the Bella before him with the girl she'd been for the last 6 months.

"Do you know any places we can go pick out a tree, or should I call Chris' assistant?" She asked practically from inside the box. Bella pulled herself out, holding a broken ornament and pouting.

Without warning, his heart raced. Bella put the ornament back in the box and pulled another from the top. Another picture and another radiant smile broke free on her face.

"Ah, I can look some up." Lucas grinned and pulled out his phone, willing his heart to slow down.

Bella slid the box into the hallway, where the light was brighter as the door to Chris' condo swung open.

"Ok, there's a place in..."

Chris stepped out in the hallway in a dashing black suit, sans tie.

Bella stood, pulling at glitter stuck to her sweater. The strange contrast between the two twins was quite pronounced. "Where are you going?"

"Meeting Kyle Devereaux at Fleur's Room. Do you want to come? Kyle..."

"You're not coming with us?" Bella shot back. "Christmas tree!"

Fresh sweat beaded along Lucas' hair and the back of his neck. *No. NO, NO, NO!*

"You two have that covered." Chris winked, sauntering to the elevator, whistling the most ANNOYING tune Lucas had ever heard. "Have fun!"

I'm going to murder him.

Lucas had no time to process Chris' utter betrayal. Phone in her hand with an outgoing call ringing, Bella used her foot and flipped the box closed.

"What are you doing?"

"Your car is too small for a tree. Calling Phil."

"Who is Phil?"

"Chris' driver."

"He's leaving."

"Yeah. He is." Her sudden laugh was so forceful that Bella snorted. "I'm going to make Phil an offer he can't refuse."

Oh...lord. THE Bella was back.

Lucas never asked how much Bella offered Phil to abandon his regular Astor passenger. But the man was waiting for them fifteen minutes later on the street in the Astor's cheapest SUV. Which was still a Mercedes SUV, but who was counting?

Chris sent many texts to both Bella and Lucas. Bella's were laced with veiled threats. Lucas' messages were filled with prodding.

Phil drove them through Manhattan, eyes flicking up to meet Lucas' eyes often and lots of messages coming through on his cell phone too. Lucas could figure out who was texting their driver so much.

With all the pressure, Lucas felt the walls closing in on him. Everyone was expecting something. Eyes watching him.

"You're unusually quiet." Bella hummed, the mischievous grin she got when tormenting her brother visible in the light of a passing car.

His phone buzzed again and there was not enough energy in the world for him to read yet another text prompting him to make his move. And now the car was stiflingly hot.

"Today was... I..."

She fiddled with the zipper on her jacket. "I hope Chris didn't pawn off work to you or Daniel for the clinic. I should have made more of the calls. Or his assistant. Or I don't know... But then mother was there and.... Ugh!"

Lucas felt like he might choke on the lump in his throat. "I offered."

"Ahem." Phil cleared his throat. They'd come to a stop at the entrance of a lot lit with strings of lights over small rows of fir trees. Bella was out the door as Phil grabbed the handle. A small cart outside the fenced-in lot, manned by a lovely woman dressed in a red and white Mrs. Clause costume, a wig of short curls and all. Lucas ordered three hot cocoas. He handed one off to Phil and held the other as he stood next to the booth at

the front. They sipped and watched, both smart enough not to get in Bella's way.

Enthralled with the trees, Bella was already hopping down the aisle, pulling out trees several feet taller than herself. The attendant on duty, a guy probably barely out of high school, tried insisting that he help Bella. Lucas tried to warn the guy, but Bella persisted. The threat of a looming slap hung in the air when the attendant attempted to help Bella hold a tree. Finally, after measuring nearly every tree in the lot, Bella chose one only slightly taller than herself. Lucas could easily touch the top without a step stool to add the star.

"You're sure you want that one?" Lucas asked after realizing he was taller than the tree.

Her smile glowed in the moonlight. "It's me sized!"

"Then it's perfect."

Bella wouldn't let anyone else pay for *her* tree, including Phil, who would have just been using Astor money anyway. The attendant was nearly thrown into oncoming traffic when Bella insisted on tying the tree down with Lucas. It wasn't their first tree wrangling. Michigan Christmases with Bella and Chris had included everything from ice fishing to obtaining an emergency Christmas Tree the day before Christmas Eve for the Holt's elderly neighbor, Mrs. Griffin. One year her grandchildren couldn't make it to Kalamazoo, so Mrs. Griffin had no reason to buy a tree until Bella found out. They spent an entire afternoon with Mrs. Griffin baking cookies, trimming the tree, etc. Lucas found Bella over at Mrs. Griffin's house, late on Christmas Eve, drunk off Mrs. Griffin's family eggnog recipe and singing Christmas carols off-pitch.

Bella stood in the back passenger doorway, tossing Lucas the other end of the rope to loop around the bottom of the tree before they tied it off. When Lucas' knot was done, he tried to see if Bella was finished, but the tree blocked his view.

He circled the SUV. Bella still stood in the doorway, yanking the knot tight. She shivered in the frigid night. With no gloves, her hands were raw and chapped. Lucas came up behind her, holding his gloves up for her to take, and placed his other hand on her back so she wouldn't fall if he startled her.

"Hey! Uh..." Bella started. Words died on her tongue.

Lucas almost let her go. They were so close, and Bella wobbled, losing her balance. She draped her arm around his neck to steady herself, but otherwise, she was speechless, eyes locked on Lucas'. His chest squeezed tight.

Quietly, Phil cleared his throat. The cars behind them were waiting for the Astor car to move so they could park close to the tree lot. Even though he thought his heart might burst, Lucas placed a hand on Bella's waist and helped her down from the doorway. Drawing her into him when he almost lost his grip. His hands held her waist, and Bella's arms lingered at his neck. Their eyes never left the others. Both were breathing hard, in sync. The world around them dimmed.

"Mr. Holt, sir?"

Phil's voice broke the spell.

"Yeah. We should..."

"... we should go." Bella straightened up, tucking Lucas' gloves in her pocket. She flashed a sheepish smile and pitched her head at the SUV.

Lucas climbed into the SUV first, flushed.

CHAPTER FIFTEEN
Lights, garland... still need a tree

Lucas

Bella stared at Lucas while keeping up a constant stream of chatter. A true comfort considering his mind and motor functions had returned to their anxiety-induced frozen state he'd spent most of high school in. It happened every time Kayla Whitworth (his longest-standing crush before Bella) walked into a room, and they shared most of their classes.

Or maybe his loss of motor function and inability to speak was more like freshman year (and every other year since) at Columbia after he met Bella. Back then, she'd latched onto him as a friend when he'd had no others. Even when Lucas had been sure Chris was going to get him thrown out of the university for looking at him the wrong way. And snorting at him on the first day of their Business 101 class. Bella befriended him.

Did Bella notice his frozen state? No. When his hearing worked properly again, he heard her talking at length about Christmas plans. The cookies they would make this year. Ice fishing, including her yearly threat of throwing Chris down the hole in the ice, etc. But, seriously, the entire time, Bella stayed turned toward him, staring and turning his brain into a puddle of mush.

In no time, Phil pulled in front of Bella's apartment building. He'd double-parked only long enough to free Bella's Christmas tree from the roof, pull out Bella's boxes from the trunk, and set them on the sidewalk.

Seconds after Phil left to find a proper parking space, Lucas realized he was alone. Phil circled the block and found a parking space several buildings away, but Bella was dragging the tree on her own into the building. Lucas snapped out of his daydreams, ran after her, and lifted the trunk off the ground.

"Bells! Wait for Phil."

"He speaks!" she said and beamed from behind the tree's branches. "Phil'll catch up." She mumbled something about the man being psychic, and he'd absorbed evil powers from her mother.

Inside the building, the tight turns pinched Lucas against the tree and wall several times until they made it to her apartment. Phil, in the unique way he'd perfected in his years of Astor family employment, appeared out of nowhere behind them. His key to Bella's apartment was ready before either of them could pull theirs out. He didn't even wither under Bella's very Astor-like glare as he held the door open for them.

"Ma'am," Phil said with a placid smile.

"I'll 'ma'am' you," Bella complained.

Lucas noted the knowing smirk Phil gave him and the ornament boxes at his feet before bidding Bella a goodnight and that he would pick her up in the morning.

"Don't you dare!" Bella threatened.

But he tipped his hat to her and bid her goodnight again, disappearing into the hallway.

Stamping her foot, Bella glared at the door. "Chris is an ass! He... he..."

He'd planned so much more than having his driver cart them around to get a Christmas tree in a romantic location.

Lucas learned to keep his mouth shut. He was certain Chris arranged for most of what had happened tonight.

A realization hit him. Lucas realized they'd been so distracted by everything that they had grabbed ornament boxes but not a tree stand. However, sitting on top of the ornament box, Phil had left a tree stand.

Bella swiped the stand, stripped off her jacket, and after they'd bolted the tree into the stand, her sweater came off too. Lucas assumed his own sweating had been because of Bella and her proximity, the way she touched his arm to get his attention to ask a question, or so on.

They'd set up the tree in the space between her television stand and the door to her bedroom. Really jamming it in. Bella lay under the tree, bolting the tree into place, creating more mushy brain in Lucas when her leg caressed his.

"I said, wiggle the tree," Bella, apparently, repeated herself with a giggle.

"Right. Yeah. Sorry," Lucas said. He wiggled the tree.

Satisfied, Bella fetched water. After a second trip under, needles from the tree caught in her hair when she crawled back out. Lithely, Bella hopped onto the couch next to Lucas, the box on the floor between them, and beamed at him.

"Well?" Bella asked. She watched him expectantly.

Oh, my god. What were we talking about?

His mind went completely blank. Lucas' only thought was to clean the pine needles out of her hair.

"You okay?" Bella asked when he said nothing.

"Uh, yeah." He gingerly reached out. Bella didn't flinch away — she never did — and pulled a needle from her hair.

"Thanks." She sent her hands through her hair and pulled a few more stuck in her now unkempt curls. "I was asking if you wanted dinner. All we've had so far is cocoa."

"Dinner?"

"Yeah! I can cook... something. We did just get groceries, and you are always making me dinner. I assume you got enough to make more than one meal."

Lucas kept staring. "Groceries?"

"My brother works you too hard." Bella's lilting laugh sent his heart fluttering. "We could order food instead. Thai? There's that new place a few blocks away. I think they're still open." Bella scooted closer to him, kicking open the ornament box. Goosebumps traced lines up her arms.

"Are you cold?" Lucas asked.

"No."

Was it his imagination, or was she scooting closer again? "Let's order. I'd rather go through ornaments with you."

Bella patted around for her phone, back pockets, and non-existent front pockets, then frowned. She shoved her hands into the gaps of the couch and came away with nothing. He didn't feel her hand slipping into his pocket and grabbing his phone until he saw it out. Bella's shoulder leaned into his, her head resting on his shoulder.

"Lucas?" she asked, her voice trailing off.

He pulled at needles trapped in her hair he hadn't seen before. She smelled of nothing but fresh-cut fir trees. Suddenly, Bella jerked up, her head smacking Lucas' jaw.

"I'll... make dinner."

"Bella?"

"It's fine." She hustled into the kitchen, tossing his phone on the couch next to him.

The air, the entire mood, shifted so suddenly Lucas was thrown off balance.

A phone call popped up on his phone. Anita Viglia. Their coordinator at Macy's for their upcoming event. Lucas groaned and moved off to Bella's bedroom to take the call.

"Director Holt," he answered, his tone clipped now. "What can I do for you, Ms. Viglia?"

"Oh, I saw you saw my text and... well, I just wanted to see if..."

"Now is not a good time. I thought we cleared up all the issues for this weekend."

"We did. We... did," Anita repeated the words, mostly to herself. All traces of the usually perky woman was gone.

"Great. Whatever it is, we can discuss it this weekend."

Anita brightened. "Okay!"

A pained sigh escaped Lucas. *What turned Bella's mood?*

Lucas couldn't imagine he'd done anything to make Bella's mood turn. That's when it hit him. Anita said text. Fuck! A text? What did she say in the text?

Anita Viglia (Macy's Contact): *Would you like to get dinner with me? Maybe after the Astor Pharm Santa's Village event? (you really need a better name for that)*

No. This wasn't happening.

Bella read this. On accident, but she read it.

Lucas' hands trembled as he rasped, "Bella?"

"Hmm?" She was sauteeing something, eyes fixed on the pan.

"It's... it's not what it looks like."

Bella's eyes met his. From across the apartment, he saw the undeniable shift in her mood. A distance they'd never had before. "You should have told me. You're always so quiet about girls you like."

"No. That's not..."

"I'm happy for you."

He needed to fix this. Words like '*I love you*' were on the tip of his tongue, but the moment was gone. And Bella would just think he was being shy or quiet and probably wouldn't take him seriously.

"Put on a movie. I'll finish dinner," Bella said, her voice frigid.

Bella

Stupid, stupid, stupid.

Bella took every one of those ridiculous emotions Alicia's ridiculous babbling brought to the surface and tried stuffing them away in a lockbox in her mind. Friends for what... 12 or 13 years now? What was wrong with her?

Yes, Lucas made her happier than anyone. When she's with him, there's a contentedness, a safety, a comfort they've always had with each other. In the night, when fear or a nightmare gripped her, Lucas held her and kept her warm. Or knew precisely what to say to calm her when she woke up...

She was being silly. He had his own life and deserved to be happy.

One more night. She could try to be normal for one more night. Forget about Christmas. Let Lucas have his date with Anita without Bella interfering. To have the chance at his life without trapping him with her.

Bella put on a smile, and they ate dinner on the couch. After dinner, they dug through their handmade Christmas ornaments, lights, and garland. And by the end, she drifted off to some holiday movie with a twinkly tree filled with the best memories, her best friend beside her.

In the morning, she'd just be Bella Astor, his friend. His completely platonic friend that no one would mistake for a girlfriend.

She wouldn't screw up his chance with Anita.

CHAPTER SIXTEEN
Red envelope

Bella

Preston Warren had held Bella in a stranglehold for so long that Bella felt the gambit of emotions without him hiding in her brain. Those emotions led to wild dreams jolting her awake every few hours. Lucas' soft words lulled her back to sleep. When they finally woke, Lucas' smile lit his entire face as he gazed down at her. His arm was comfortably around her back, keeping her safe.

Bella let out a sigh, and an emptiness in her grew. This had to end if Lucas was going to start dating someone.

"Are you okay?" Lucas asked and brushed the hair from her cheek.

"Yeah," Bella broke free. "Busy day."

Because if she stayed busy, had enough excuses, and kept herself away from him and let him have his date, his life. All the things he gave up for her since she'd returned home. In her life, Bella had seen too many people give up too much for the Astor family. She wouldn't let Lucas give up on a happy life.

But tearing herself from Lucas' side was like ripping a band-aid off a wound four times the bandage's size.

She kept telling herself, *Be happy for him. Be glad Lucas is going on a date and getting himself out there.*

Her body didn't get the freaking memo.

Lucas dropped her at the clinic to oversee the cleanup. She blushed.

Lucas texted her. A fire burned everywhere in her.

Called her? Forget it. She refused to answer because even her mind ground to a halt.

Bella didn't remember ever blushing so much for anyone. Not for Preston or any guys she dated in high school. And she dated no one during her undergrad degree.

It was utterly ridiculous, and the only explanation had to be Bella was amid a rebound she never expected. Closure with Preston and making sure her best friend could find someone that made him happy was just emotional fucking things screwing her up. Space and time away from Lucas would help.

However, there was no way to avoid Lucas for too long. The Astor Pharmaceutical Santa's Village (Lucas needed to come up with a better name) program started bright and... well, at mid-day on Saturday. Bella had only a day of avoiding Lucas until she couldn't.

Of course, when Saturday morning rolled around, Bella was a mess. Half-formed curls, frizz, and whatever was going on with her makeup. Somehow, she was convinced that nearly five years away made her 'out of practice' with doing her hair. She called Alicia, shouting emergency, and Alicia rushed over.

"Girl, how is this an emergency for Bella effing Astor? Do you remember when we'd go out to clubs?"

"You mean eight years ago when paparazzi literally followed me everywhere?"

"What did you do to your hair?" Alicia's fingers stuck in the tangles Bella had created.

Of course, Alicia's stunning black hair glistened, sleek and straight today. Utterly and stunningly perfect. They wore matching green and white dresses embroidered with glittery snowflakes and trimmed in white faux fur.

Alicia glanced at the slightly jagged scar running along Bella's collarbone. "You sure you want to wear this dress?"

Bella shrugged. Tabloids were already saying the meanest, shittiest things they could think of. *If* anything happened today for them to write a new article about Bella Astor, her scar was the least of Bella's worries. Everyone worried so much about the line across her collarbone, but when Bella saw it in the mirror...

Well, for as downright terrifying as that day was, for as many nightmares, jumps, and scares that sent her heart racing, her scar was physical proof she'd done some good in her life.

Lucas

On Friday, every text Lucas sent Bella took forever to get a response, if he got one at all. It was for the best when she'd finally told him she needed extra sleep that night. Lucas needed time to plan how to tell Bella what he felt. Sadly, the process took hours of pacing, ripping at his hair, and berating himself since each idea seemed dumber than the last.

Well past midnight, Lucas switched gears and packed a bag of arts and crafts supplies he donated as something extra for the

Astor Pharm event. Bright red construction paper sat on top. Silver pens...

And the idea hit him.

Five drafts later, Lucas had a passable, if somewhat rambling, letter confessing his love for Bella.

Not daring to mess up the letter with some fancy folding, he folded it into quarters and tied a sparkly silver ribbon around like a gift.

Bella

"That suit looks good on Lucas," Alicia cooed in Bella's ear.

They sat in the back of the bus, playing with a couple of toddlers, letting their moms have a moment's rest.

Oh, lord! Was it hot on the bus heading to Macy's?

Kids chattered, sang, and screamed along with their parents and babies. Three busloads of people. Why — *why* — did she get on the same bus as both Lucas and Alicia?

"I didn't notice."

She did *not* notice the pale gray twill suit and Santa hat tie he wore. A suit he'd bought after her father extended an offer to Lucas before he started senior year at Columbia. And a tie Bella gave him two years before she entered Frontier Doctors. Nope, she did not notice at all.

The entire morning instantly became a second-guessing game. Bella checked her hair in the bus window reflection, her makeup too. Was her black peacoat closed or open? Which looked better?

Did she look like she was having a panic attack about every little detail for no stupid reason? The answer had to be yes. Everyone was being kind and ignored her.

Lucas meandered up and down the aisle, talking to parents and kids, even stopping at one of Bella's patients, Callie, and signing her hot pink arm cast.

Luck was not on Bella's side. Neither was Alicia. Every stoplight turned red, and every street was jammed up, keeping them on the bus longer and giving Bella fewer reasons to not notice Lucas. Especially when he picked up the toddler next to her, slapped her arm, sat him on his lap, and winked. When they arrived, Lucas held a hand to Bella and Alicia, offering to walk them in.

A rush of delighted squeals drowned out the Christmas music as soon as the elevator doors opened on the eighth floor of Macy's. From their vantage point, Santaland had a corridor roped off for children to stand in line while an entire North Pole village surrounded them. Trees, 'snow,' walls brightly painted with buildings like Santa's Workshop and more. Macy's employees, dressed as Santa's elves, waved at the kids. Before the kids hit Santaland, kid-sized tables, chairs, and craft supplies were out. And set up on the far edges were more tables set up with steaming silver buffet dishes. Macy's wasn't closed for the day, obviously, since this was their biggest shopping season. But most of the floor was inaccessible to patrons for the day. Astor family politics at work.

The next elevator load of children and parents opened behind them, and even more delighted squeals drowned whatever coherent thoughts Bella had out. Some kids dragged Alicia off to draw at a nearby table.

"What do you think?" Lucas asked, hands out, offering to take her jacket.

For the first time since seeing the text from Melissa on Lucas' phone, Bella locked eyes with Lucas, feeling her own well. "It's perfect."

Reluctantly, Bella let go of his arm and shrugged out of her coat, and Lucas took it, continuing to say hello to parents and kids as he passed them. Somehow, she never realized how many of her patients and parents Lucas had gotten to know in the last year.

"Isn't this quaint?"

Her skin prickled at Preston's voice behind her.

Bella forced a tiny smile. "It's wonderful. What are you doing here? Trying to ruin it?"

"I'm legal counsel for..." Bella moved closer, stomping down where she thought his foot might be, and missed. "You're predictable, Bella."

She wheeled on him, but Preston stood firm. Holding out an envelope. "I needed to deliver this. From my father. For Christian and *Holt*."

He waved the envelope a few times before Bella snatched it, trying to make the cocky smirk disappear.

Usually, that never works. Today, however, Preston's face tightened. Even sagged a little, but he said, "You look stunning." And gave her a wary once over.

"You always hated my festive dresses."

"No. That's not true."

His eyes didn't lie. Preston couldn't hold her gaze for long, and when he tried, he looked down past her face at the white fur trim and balled up his hands.

"Whatever," Bella muttered and turned. Preston caught her arm, but too late.

A woman stopped Lucas. Petite, dressed as an elf like the other Macy's employees. Short brown hair cut in a bob. Another girl with an athletic build, like Bella used to have. Like his last girlfriend, Nora. Lucas never showed Bella a picture, but Chris had.

Melissa's hand slid up Lucas' arm as she moved closer. Lucas smiled down at her.

They were cute together.

"Come on." Preston nudged her back. "Come here. I have something for you."

Bella felt a hollowness inside grow and let Preston usher her out of the deafening room.

Lucas

"So, dinner? Tonight?" Melissa's wide smile pained Lucas.

"I can't," he said, trying to disentangle himself from Melissa's grasp.

"But I thought..."

Lucas took her hand off his arm gently and drew away.

His stomach churned, and he questioned if he could say the words without throwing up. After a moment, he blurted out, "I don't have feelings for you, Melissa."

"Oh," Melissa said. "I'm sorry."

"I should have made it clear sooner." His stomach still rebelled, but Lucas finished with something he never thought he'd say. "I have feelings for someone else."

Melissa assured Lucas several times that she was okay. She was not upset, though her pain was plain as day.

He took three whole steps when Alicia got in his way and demanded, "Where's Bella?"

"She's right," Lucas said and pointed near the elevator, where he'd left Bells, but there was nothing but a sea of kids and parents.

"What were you just doing?" She twisted his finger painfully. "Flirting?"

"Telling Melissa I didn't have feelings for her."

She let his finger go, and it throbbed.

"I swear to God, that woman is finally realizing what you mean to her, and if you screw it up..."

"I might have already." Lucas moaned.

"What?" Alicia's shriek brought more attention than Lucas wanted.

"I think Bells saw a text from Melissa, and I couldn't tell her..."

"You are your own worst enemy. Chris said you have a plan."

"What does Chris know?"

Alicia glared a glare worthy of Mrs. Lina Astor that made Lucas feel like a child in trouble again.

"I'm going to find her, and I'm going to tell her," he said, giving the breast pocket on his suit a pat.

"I'm so stupidly invested in this. Make it work! That an engagement ring in there?"

"No."

"Lame. You should straight up propose at this point."

Bella

"Are you doing okay?" Preston asked after he hauled her back behind Santaland to an employee-only hallway and plucked the handkerchief from his jacket pocket.

"Fine!" Bella snapped.

"Of course, Bella Astor doesn't cry." Preston grinned and stuffed the handkerchief back into his pocket.

"Not in front of assholes like you."

He scoffed but said nothing. With his hands stuffed into his pants pockets, Pres leveled his rich worry-filled eyes on her. Almost like he still cared about Bella.

"It's nothing, Pres. I'm fine." Bella pulled herself up, back straight. Bella sighed, fiddling with her hair and pulling on a section until the curl fell flat.

The woody notes and contrasting sharp spice, like cloves, hit Bella. Preston's signature scent. The cologne he must bathe in. The smell brought warmth to her.

Preston closed the gap, enveloping her in his scent and arms, pulling her into him. "Talk to me."

"You'll think it's dumb."

"You are quite literally the smartest woman I have ever known."

Lucas

No one saw Bella after they arrived at Santaland. No one saw her disappear. She was just gone.

The line to talk to Santa wrapped around all the craft tables while parents sat with hot cocoa and picked at the buffet.

Melissa mentioned there was a way behind Santa's seating area that led to Santa's changing and break area. Lucas didn't wait for her to finish before cutting through the line of kids. He hopped over the red velvet rope barrier and searched for the hallway among the wooden Santa's village buildings and Christmas trees. He found the break-in buildings and saw a long white wall. The hallway to the break room.

When he peered around the corner into the hallway, Lucas caught Preston pressing a kiss on Bella's forehead. Her cheeks were bright pink and her chest was heaving.

Not again.

CHAPTER SEVENTEEN
Gut instinct

Bella

Preston left Bella standing in the hallway without another word. Her skin tingled where his lips pressed into her forehead, and the envelope clutched in her hand.

When her world stopped spinning, Bella returned to Santa, his village, and the kids and tried to act normal. And she ran straight into Lucas, who hadn't put her coat away yet. She'd taken her jacket back for something to do. As well as something to pull and tug on when her thoughts turned right back to Pres.

No! I spent so much time getting over that asshole! And I finally did it.

Hours passed by making crafts, talking with parents, and hearing from the kids what they wanted for Christmas.

At the end, Lucas' big reveal stunned the crowd. He returned with Santa and bags of gifts. Kids rushed the pair, but Santa got their attention. Lucas waded through the kids and handed out gifts with Santa. Paper went flying. Squeals of delight filled the room even louder than when they'd first arrived.

And Lucas, for his part, seemed thrilled.

Bella ached watching him. His sweet smile sliced deeper each time she saw it. She needed to escape. Wrapped in her coat, squeezing it tight, Bella rode down to the first floor and stepped onto the packed afternoon sidewalk. Shoppers bitched and moaned that she was in their way, but Bella needed space and time. She stepped out of the iconic glass doorway and shivered under the first awning for the windows.

Be happy. Be happy.

She clung to the chant.

"Hey, you."

"Why are you stalking me, Preston?" Bella asked. She took one step onto the sidewalk, and people complained; Preston blocked foot traffic

and no one batted an eye.

Preston jabbed a finger towards his car and asked, "Need a breather?"

"Not with you."

"It'll be worth it."

No, it would not be worth it. Because nothing with Preston had ever been worth the pain afterward. Strictly speaking, that wasn't an entirely accurate statement.

"Come on. I'm not trying to seduce you."

"As if you could anymore."

"That, Miss Astor, sounds like a challenge."

"It's not a challenge."

"I could take it as one." Preston stepped up within inches of her, took a lock of her hair, and gave it a couple gentle tugs. That sent her heart into flutters in the past, but not now. "Promise it will be the most perfect five minutes. Ten, at most. Then I'll drop you back off here. No one will be the wiser."

She'd heard that before.

Stupid. Why did Bella get in Preston's car?

And why did she ask such *stupid* questions when she knew exactly why. Each little glance stolen by Melissa and Lucas was another stab in her chest.

ARGH!

Bella didn't recognize Preston's driver today. He was quiet, and his hat was drawn down, hiding his face. Was he refusing to look her in the eye? Then once in the driver's seat, he was hidden behind a window separating them. Indeed, Bella was alone with Preston Warren.

Well, Bella Astor was known for her idiotic decisions, so this newest stupid decision shouldn't come as a surprise to anyone. And who knows? Maybe her mother would catch a glimpse of Bella on the cover of another tabloid and a ridiculous article about her and Preston reconciling.

The drive was short, just to Rockefeller Center and its towering Christmas tree and skating rink, packed with more crowds than Macy's.

Preston opened his door and held his hand out for her, waiting. Resolute, Bella blew out a puff of air and folded her arms over her chest.

"You'll only get angry if *he* opens the door for you, so...?"

Wow. It was as if Preston actually had listened to her all those years they'd known each other.

"What are we doing here?"

"A breather. Like I said."

"There are more people here than at Macy's."

Truly. People packed into the iconic skating rink and crowded around the sidewalks. Children ran among the trees and decorations, dragging their parents by the hand. No snow fell, but low-hanging clouds threatened another coating for New Yorkers to slip and slide on.

She should get back to their Astor Pharmaceutical event, but...

"Come on. Real quick." Preston walked ahead of her towards the tree. "Then you can have fun playing Santa's elf," he teased.

"I'm a cute elf!"

An abrupt stop on Preston's part ran Bella right into his back. He turned to catch her, his rich dark brown eyes grabbing her attention. Warm and captivating.

"Most beautiful—"

"Don't!" Bella snarled and pushed him onward. "Just show me whatever you wanted to—"

But Pres moved too slowly for her. She jostled past then it was her turn to stop.

At the base of the iconic tree, one of her patients, a little boy named Max, with thick straight brown hair cut short, leaped into the arms of an older man. His mother, Jenny, clutched a baby to her chest. Max's dad had been deployed; there was no chance for leave, yet here he was.

"They were supposed to be at your little event thing, but father and I didn't want to take away from the other kids' moments." Preston lightly placed his hands on her shoulders. "And the tree here is a bit more magical."

"What? How?"

"Doesn't matter how." Preston gathered her blond curls and dropped them over one shoulder. He leaned in and whispered in her ear, "Merry Christmas."

Horrible mistake. Mistake to end all mistakes.

What in the name of all things holy and sacred had Bella been thinking?

Short answer, she hadn't.

Long answer... this gave her a reason to let Lucas have room to make a life. His life.

Bella let Preston sleep as she got out of his bed, slipped on her shoes, and left his condo.

Lucas

Early Sunday morning, before Lucas had time to finish his coffee, Chris had complained so much Lucas' ear might fall off.

"Bella's not stupid."

Sunday work was a rare occurrence, but all the directors worked overtime ahead of the holidays to shore up the loose ends with current shipping crises, manufacturing crises, and more before heading home for the holidays. If Lucas worked at most companies, he'd probably be on vacation. Still, he couldn't leave this mess behind for Bella's father, Eli. Even if Eli wasn't with them anymore, he would disapprove. Eli Astor would have stayed to get the work done.

"I literally know that," Lucas complained right back.

"You *literally* don't."

"I'm fixing it. I already talked to Melissa!"

"You NEED TO TALK TO BELLA." Chris jumped on Lucas and started ripping reports out of his hand. "I'm going to fire you if you don't!"

Lucas tried to channel Chris and Bella's mom with his intense glare.

"Fine, I won't fire you, but come on! This is the *most painful thing* I have ever witnessed!"

In a rare moment, Chris looped his arm around Lucas' neck in an attempt at a headlock. It was weak and nothing like wrestling. Certainly no power behind the move like his sister.

"Just... freaking..."

"Uh? Hi, Bella!" Lucas choked on the last word as Chris squeezed.

Bella and Melissa stood in Lucas' office doorway. Chris immediately let go and stood to fix his shirt and flip his floppy curls to the opposite side.

Bella said, "I don't even want to know." More to herself than anyone else.

"What are you doing here?" Chris asked, turning his potent gaze to Melissa and giving her a thorough once over.

Bella held up a crushed envelope. "Met *Melissa* at security when I was coming in. Here." She tossed the envelope to her brother. "From Preston's father. I'll be on my way."

"No!" Chris and Lucas screamed.

Bella froze and shrugged. "It's fine. Melissa has *stuff* to discuss and... I'm busy."

"B-busy?" Lucas stuttered.

Bella

Busy screwing up her own life. Because agreeing to lunch with Preston was the icing on the 'fuck up Bella's life' cake.

But each time Melissa yanked her shirt straight or primped her hair Bella knew she was doing the right thing for someone. The someone just wasn't Bella.

"Yeah," Bella said, fighting to keep her voice level. "You boys are busy fixing stuff for the company. Don't need me underfoot."

Launching himself across the room, Chris grabbed Bella around the waist. "You, my dearest sister, have always been better at business-related... crap."

"Crap?" Bella smiled smugly.

"Stay? Help... Lucas?" Chris' voice became pathetic and whiny. Her brother was actually pleading. "You're better at this stuff than either of us."

"I was better at plant design, not shipping or customs or whatever Lucas is fixing. Also, can't. Busy. Ish. Anyway, Melissa needed to talk to Lucas. So..."

Bella shouldered Chris off her and didn't bother saying anything else, just tilting her head at the silent girl standing patiently in Lucas' doorway.

"Bye," Bella ground out. "Good luck."

What remained of a smile on her lips wavered.

Lucas

The bounce in Bella's step was undeniable, yet something was off with Bella. Something Lucas couldn't quite put his finger on. Her eyes? Her stance? Definitely her smile. It was all reminiscent of something he'd seen before.

Chris smashed his face into Lucas' channeling an incorrigible twelve-year-old kid. "She will never know unless you grow some balls and tell her."

Scratch that. He was channeling a six-year-old. Flicking at Lucas' hair until Lucas couldn't stand it any longer.

Melissa giggled, pausing Chris from attacking again.

"I get it now," she said. "You *should* tell her."

A gasp echoed from the elevator. Lucas and Chris fought for who got to his door first. Melissa flattened herself against the wall to avoid being tackled.

"I knew it," Lucas said as a strangled sound came from his throat.

Voluntarily hanging out with Preston after such a public fight always made her act weird. That look in her eye, that off feeling.

"Knew what?" Chris asked.

"She slept with Warren."

"*She slept with Pres?* And you? You're just going to let her walk away. My dumbass sister will screw up her life, and *you*'ll let her do it?"

Bella's own words played on repeat.

"You should ask her out."

"She seems pretty."

Preston fixed a lock of Bella's hair. First gut punch. She smiled up at him. Second gut punch.

But it wasn't what Lucas would call a 'happy smile.' Which tore at him even more.

"She'll figure it out," Lucas whispered.

"Just go out there and tell her."

"Do you pay attention to your sister?"

"You won't ever know if you don't. I keep telling you this! She thinks you want to date M... m... I'm sorry. What was your name again?"

Lucas answered for her. "Melissa." Then immediately apologized. "Sorry. You can answer for yourself."

Of course – of course! – Melissa blushed at him.

"Waiting won't fix this situation! It requires action. Stop Bella from going out with Preston."

"It does require action," Lucas agreed.

Chris would never like the action it required. Waiting and being there for Bella. Being the best friend he was to her. That was more important than telling her. Because thrusting his feelings on her, cornering her never worked to anyone's advantage.

Plus, something about Bella, something he'd never seen her do before, told him to wait.

And, for as painful as it was, Lucas would stand by her.

Lucas crashed onto his couch, too tired to make dinner. When a text popped up, he thought about texting Bella to find out if she wanted to meet at her place and have dinner.

Bella: *I think I made a mistake.*

Lucas: *I'm sure you didn't*

Bullshit. This was going to do with Preston, and anything with that man was a mistake. Not that he would say that.

Bella: *Preston asked me to accompany him to my mother's gala.*

Gala. Her *mother's* gala?

Lucas: Isn't that the same night as the party at the community center?

Bella: I'll be at both? I'll only stay at mother's for an hour. Tops.

Bella: Am I making a mistake?

The answer was obvious.

His mind screamed *just say yes! Yes, it's a mistake.*

But another part of his mind told him to take a breath. Wait.

Lucas: I'll help you get ready

The folded letter he meant to give Bella at yesterday's event sat on his glass coffee table, the ribbon untied. He'd found the letter still in his jacket that morning and read it once he was alone in his office.

Bella: You didn't answer my question

Lucas: It's not a mistake if you want to go with him

She typed for a while. Bubbles dancing on the screen.

Bella: Is Melissa going to be at the community center?

Lucas: No

Bella: But she asked you out

Bella: She's gorgeous, you dummy

The letter he'd written taunted him. Nudged him to say,

Lucas: So are you

He pulled out the leftover construction paper and the silver paint pen and began rewriting the letter. Bella deserved better than what he'd written the first time.

CHAPTER EIGHTEEN
DO NOT RIP THE VERSACE DRESS!!!!

Lucas

Barely a few hours of sleep after finishing his revised letter to Bella and Lucas woke to a string of texts pinging his phone. Lucas rubbed his eyes and attempted to blink the blurriness away. Annoyingly, it wouldn't go away. Finally, Lucas realized he had slept in his contacts.

Once in his glasses, he squinted at texts; each became bolder, more emojis and pleading for Lucas to 'get his ass to B's place.' Another dropped down from the top of his phone while he read.

Alicia: Seriously, dude! 911! Get over here!

Lucas went in search of Chris and answers, except Chris wasn't in his condo or answering his phone. Whatever had happened, Lucas was moving sluggish enough that he needed coffee before attempting to intervene in matters of Bella, no matter what the emergency was. Nothing too terrible could have happened if no one had mentioned the police.

Once dressed in his regular work attire, black slacks and white oxford, Lucas pulled out a Christmas tree tie Bella's father gifted Lucas the year before his passing. He slung the tie around his neck without tying, then stashed the new letter for Bella in his jacket pocket. Lucas was ready to tackle whatever the emergency was once he filled a thermos with enough coffee to start a small side business.

Finding a parking spot near Bella's apartment took longer than the drive, but finally, he was at her door and digging out his key. A wild string of profanities came through the door.

"Bells? Why am I getting 911 texts from you and 'Licia..." Lucas jammed his shoulder into the door and crashed into a rack of dresses covered in bags.

Alicia spared no time in digging into him. "Because it's a God damn emergency! That's why!"

Lucas used one finger and pushed a dress along the rack until he saw the label on the next. Oscar de la Renta. Promptly, he pulled his hand away and backed into Bella's kitchen, dropping the thermos of coffee safely away from dresses worth months of salary.

"What is going on?"

From her bedroom, Bella shouted loud enough to startle her brother out of the room. "What in the ever-loving fuck is this shit?"

"Bella! Do *not* rip the Versace! Do not!" Alicia rounded the rack, advancing on Lucas. "Lina fucking found out Preston asked B to the Astor Gala, and she cornered Bella last night when we were cleaning the clinic!"

Lucas' body went numb. Bella hadn't answered his last text, leaving it on read all night. He assumed she didn't know what to say. That this was the perfect time to give her the letter.

It was not.

"Lina never steps foot in the clinic," he said.

"She stepped more than a foot in the clinic last night," Alicia continued, hardly audible over Bella's next rant.

"Shit." Which felt like an understatement to end all understatements.

"We cannot keep her calm. She's going to destroy those dresses. And her mother expects her at the gala on Preston's damn arm! All lovey-fucking-dovey!"

"I'm with Alicia. Get your ass in there." Chris slapped a few dresses to the side. He yanked one off the rack in a black plastic bag and held it out for Lucas to take in with him. "We've tried everything, and it's not working."

"Save us, Lucas." Alicia deadpanned the famous line. "You're our only hope."

Declining the dress, Lucas stepped into Bella's bedroom doorway. A simple full bed, dresser, and nightstand, all in matching dark black wood, offset with vibrant blue and green sheets. Folded on the foot of the bed was the second t-shirt blanket Bella made from Lucas' old high school t-shirts. In the corner, between the dresser and a tall window, Bella growled at her reflection in the standing mirror.

A cape of black satin draped gracefully to the floor, covered in dazzling crystals glinting like stars against the dark velvet of night. Bella whipped around, the dress just as stunning as the cape. Twinkling and hugging her curves gracefully.

Staunch anger on Bella's face didn't bring reality back to the fog inhabiting Lucas' mind as it should.

Alicia shouted again, "Don't rip the damn dress, Bella!"

"Where's a different one? Short sleeves? Nothing that will fucking strangle me!" Bells yanked at the collar and turned in circles, trying for the zipper.

"They're all long sleeves, high collars." Chris drolled.

"Fuck!"

"You look..." Lucas mumbled incoherently.

"I *look* like a starry night painting vomited on me and is trying to strangle me."

Not how Lucas would describe her. It was easy to forget that Bella's beauty was natural, even when she didn't think it was. She'd done nothing with her hair. It was down with a wave and a few curls, no makeup. All the same, Lucas could hardly breathe, think... anything.

"I'm just done! I'm fucking..." Bella dug at the zipper until Lucas jumped in and stopped her from undressing in front of him.

His hand slid over hers, against her ribs, and finally ended her tirade.

"What happened?"

"I... I... was going to call Preston. Call off going to the gala because... I don't know. I just..."

Lucas brought his hands first to her shoulders, then tucked hair behind both of her ears.

"But *mother* found out and insists I need to fix all these stupid mistakes I've made lately. And this was the *perfect fucking* opportunity because it will be public and the people we know and..."

There was a big 'and' coming.

"And?" Lucas prompted.

"She threatened the future of the clinic."

"Of course she did."

Classic Lina Astor. The board of directors would do her bidding no matter what Chris argued as Astor Pharm's CEO.

Bella smashed into Lucas' chest, hugging him and hiding any new tears. So he wrapped her in his arms, resting his chin on top of her head.

"One night..." he whispered.

Bella jumped into his chin at the first buzz of his phone. He pulled it out to silence the call when the world fell away.

"I need to take this."

Wiping her face, Bella pushed onto her tiptoes. "Mother?"

Lina Astor's name in big blocky letters scrolled along the top of his screen.

"If I don't take this, your mother will have me tied to cement and dropped in the Hudson."

"She would not. Let me!"

"NO!"

Lucas didn't bother fighting. Once he was free of Bella, he stumbled from her bedroom.

Chris and Alicia stood watching from the dress rack. Lucas made a beeline for the exercise room behind the kitchen with Bella on his heels. Even under threat of bodily harm, Alicia stepped in Bella's path.

"Hello, Ms. Astor," Lucas answered on the last ring.

"Mr. Holt!" Bella's mother instilled a deep-rooted fear even in answering the phone. "I will make this succinct. You will not be in attendance at the Astor Gala."

"Excuse me?"

"Nothing is to interfere with Bella setting her future right."

"Bella's... future?" Lucas felt confusion, anger, and a sudden spike of sadness burned his lungs. "Bella is the one in control of her future."

"It's laughable that you or she ever thought that." Then Lina's tone turned gentler, which somehow sounded more frigid than any other woman Lucas had ever met. "Security for the event has been informed. You're not to *step foot inside* the Astor Manor."

The call cut off. Lucas' stomach hardened. Bella stood in the doorway, with her sparkling black gown, taking huge gasping breaths.

It's just one night.

The words rang in his mind as much now as they did every time her parents forced Bella to galas or balls during their early college years. All in search of a husband.

Bella, the woman he met back in college, who made it her mission to make headlines to get her way, sneered through drying tears.

"Alicia, we're going shopping."

"B?"

Lucas flipped around as Bella contorted to unzip the dress and start dropping it off her shoulders.

"An Astor Gala is a night no one ever forgets." Bella sighed. Cloth rustled, and a second later, her bedroom door slammed shut.

Chris moaned, "A night no one forgets?" After, he shouted, "Preston didn't do anything this time. Leave him out of it."

Bella threw the door open again, standing in her bra and half-zipped jeans, and said, "I'll be perfectly cordial."

CHAPTER NINETEEN
Stuffed into a mold

Lucas

"Based on the amount of time I spent in that damn boutique, you all better appreciate how fine Bella looks."

"'Licia? Why did you call again?" Lucas shoved his shoulder into Bella's apartment door. Bella had texted he could let himself in. Since he was already running late, he wanted to see Bella before she was whisked off in her chariot — er, mother's town car — and tortured for the evening.

Not more than a step inside Bella's apartment, Lucas' phone tumbled out of his hand, ripping the corded earpiece. Bella stood in her bedroom doorway in a heart-stopping emerald green strapless ballgown. Satin glistened in the light, shifting from emerald to almost black. The designer cut the flared skirt with a slit that reached mid-thigh on one side, and yes, her leg was peeking through. Across the bodice, silver snowflakes were embroidered, and crystals glittered like falling snow, stealing Lucas' breath from him.

Large, bouncy blonde curls cascaded over Bella's shoulder, neatly tied to one side.

Words, thoughts, everything failed Lucas. Tiny voices shouted from Lucas' phone, but he couldn't take his eyes off Bella.

"Daniel's here. I promise not more than an hour there." Bella rushed past the couch, hopping on one foot to get one more strappy silver heal on her bare foot.

She collided with Lucas, grabbing hold for balance.

"Well?" Bella beamed.

"You... look..."

Chris and Alicia's tiny voices continued from the phone. Loathe to let Bella go, Lucas did only to scoop up the phone and end the call. But his eyes never left her.

"Was that my dumbass brother?"

"Wow." Words finally caught up, which was the absolute best he could do.

Bella held each of his arms as if she needed something or someone to keep her balance, but she didn't. She was steady as a rock.

"Do you like it?" Her cheeks flushed.

They were standing so close, Bella gripping his arms tighter. Lucas refused to let go of this moment. They *could* just stay there, forget both parties.

"An hour. Tops. Then the drive back to the recreational center, and I'm all yours. Well, not all yours, but... you know. For the kids."

"The kids," Lucas mimicked. His mind was still stupidly stuck.

"Ms. Astor?" Daniel, for some unknown and ungodly reason, asked from the door.

That, finally, brought Lucas' wits back. "Will he ever learn he's not your driver anymore?"

"Daniel isn't actually driving. But he wanted to escort me." A hiccough sounded in her throat.

It took all his willpower not to grab hold of her waist and pull Bella into him.

That wobble in her voice was what she got when thinking about Eli. Her father.

All he could do was break the spell gently. "Don't be too harsh on your mother."

A wan smile spread across her face. "I just want autonomy over my life. To make my own decisions. She doesn't get to choose who I want to be with. Or what happens with my clinic," Bella said, the wobble still there but also something else. She hid her face by moving in to fix his tie side to side.

"Bella?" Lucas asked, his breath stolen away the closer she moved.

"Ms. Astor?" Daniel asked again. "We'll be unfashionably late..."

"Coming, Daniel." Bella took a step back, giving Lucas a satisfied smile now. "You look good, Holt."

Bella walked to the door without waiting for an answer, grabbing a wrap for her shoulders.

"Bella, this isn't finishing school or whatever. You have autonomy. You have a choice."

"Do I?"

Did she? Or did Bella always have to tiptoe around everyone's wishes, desires, and worst, the media?

"If you need me," Lucas heard her pause at the door and added, "I'm a text away."

Bella

The wrap warmed Bella's shoulders, but overall the chill in her never truly went away, even in the warm car. The last warmth Bella felt was standing with Lucas in her apartment. A warmth that drew her in closer to Lucas by the second. Ugh! She did not want to be here!

"Mr. Warren will meet you at the door to escort you in. There's a reporter from..." Bella waved off Daniel's instructions.

"I'm not giving an interview. I'm not bothering with *mother's* plans for me."

Daniel knew enough to end the conversation there. He set down his phone and gave her an appraising look, and an uncharacteristic sigh escaped.

"What is it?" she asked.

Daniel always had a warm smile for the twins. Bella always assumed that was because he was also a father and very fatherly with them when they were children. But at no time did she expect him to say, "Your father would be proud."

That came out of nowhere.

"I'm sure he wouldn't be if he knew..."

"Bella."

Her heart skipped a beat. In all her years knowing Daniel as her driver, caretaker, assistant, and now as a director at Astor Pharm, he'd never used her first name. Or if he did, it was accompanied by a 'miss' ahead of it.

A new stinging, more itchy and watery than earlier when she'd been waiting on Lucas clawed at her eyes. Bella didn't think she could handle Daniel continuing.

"He was always proud of you."

"Yes," Bella sighed, shoving the tears away. "So proud when I was arrested."

"Yes," Daniel countered. "Even when you were arrested."

Bella scoffed, though it was admittedly half-hearted. No one was proud when she was arrested.

"Eli raised a young woman who could and can stand independently. And when no one stood up for her, she stood up for herself."

"I was fed up with the bullshit, Daniel. Still am. And no matter how much I stand up for myself, I'm still at the beck and call of my mother. Of mother's peers. The board. The rest of the fucking world." She pulled the wrap tighter around her. "I feel like I'm being stuffed back into the shit-show mother always wanted. Like I'm a child again. No matter how hard I fight, I will never be in control."

"Is that so?"

"I mean, my mother still has this grand view of who I should marry, just like my grandfather. Marry someone like Preston. An excellent family, someone in our circle that we can make a political match and..." The hiccough in her words accompanied a glance at Daniel, who did nothing but sit there, placidly staring forward. Most of the fight drained out of Bella. "She's absolutely over the moon about Pres and me, and heaven forbid I don't fall in line with that! And if I don't, what? My clinic is going to be pulled right out from under me? All I can be is who my mother wants me to be with my own flair just to annoy the shit out of her. But I can't be... me."

"Flair?" Daniel smirked, though the shadow in the town car hid it well. "The Bella I knew before did not allow for herself to be placed in a mold. She broke through them. Ransacked meetings with her father and showed up the directors with more intuitive insights for Astor Pharmaceuticals than any man in the room."

"I was not kicked out of those meetings because I was my father's daughter. I didn't know my place."

"I think you always knew your place. Your place should have been CEO of Astor Pharm."

"That was never my place."

"Maybe. Or maybe it was never the best placement for you. But alas, your grandfather is not with us any longer. Despite what you thought, you were carving her own path even back then. Not the one your grandfather or mother wanted. I miss that Bella Astor. Though I get glimpses now and then. After everything stuffed way down has built up enough pressure to burst."

"I've changed. Everyone changes, Daniel. I had to 'grow up.'"

Picking a piece of her skirt between two fingers, Bella rolled the satin back and forth. She changed before Frontier Doctors, sure. But Bella also learned plenty of lessons during her time in the doctor's program. She'd been trying to stay in line and quietly deal with things until... until she couldn't any longer.

Daniel nodded slowly. "Yes, of course, Miss Astor. Forgive me. You may have grown out of the mold-breaking, miss, and prefer hiding away. Denying us the grace that is Miss Bella Astor in full."

"No... that's not what I meant."

But Daniel kept barreling on. "We *do* change and are never the same as we once were. But — tell me if I'm overstepping my bounds — *I* believe that piece is still inside Bella. Wanting to emerge. Something has been holding it — you — back. Whether that's fear or stress or coping with what happened in Frontier Doctors — or all of it combined. But what do I know? I am an old man who has worked for the Astor family my entire career."

"Daniel..."

The car eased to a stop so gracefully that Bella didn't notice it. She only knew when her driver silently opened the door as Daniel said, "We've arrived, Miss Astor."

Bella hadn't time to work through what Daniel said.

Daniel, his wrinkles deeper than she remembered. More gray than black in his hair. When did that happen?

As she gazed at Daniel, somewhat in shock, his eyebrow quirked up, and Daniel asked, "Would you care for me to escort you to the door?"

Bella peered out the open door at the Astor brownstone, or more accurately, a collection of several brownstones renovated and opened to one another. Mainly the building kept its structure inside with many archways and doorways among the rooms. The one exception was that several rooms had been opened up to create a modest ballroom. It surprised Bella that her mother would host a gala in their smaller (for a family like the Astor's) Brooklyn home instead of the mansion.

Next to Bella's driver, Preston stood ready, his tuxedo tailored to perfection. The kind of fit where Bella could see Preston's athletic build underneath all the layers without much imagination. He'd combed his dark hair back, but a wave persisted. And a solitary piece tried to break away and fall to the side. His hand held out for her; Preston waited patiently for Bella to make the first move.

Daniel cleared his throat, and she jumped. "No, Daniel. Thank you."

"Have a lovely evening, Miss Astor."

"Quit with the Miss Astor bullshit, Daniel. You already called me Bella."

His smile warmed, reaching all the way to his eyes even in the dark of the town car. "I'd be loathed to call you as such, Miss Astor."

"You don't work for my mother in that capacity anymore, *Daniel*," Bella hissed as she slid out of the car.

Stepping from the town car, though, a weight lifted from Bella. Something she hadn't known she'd been holding onto.

An onslaught of flashes from photographers on the sidewalk twinkled, and faceless reporters and paparazzi vied for position.

This was why her mother rarely had galas or large social functions in the city. Or maybe it was *precisely* why she was this time.

"So, B?"

She glowered at Preston. Five seconds and he was pushing her buttons.

"What's the plan?"

"What makes you think I have a plan?" she folded her arms, and more flashes blinded her. But she would rather freeze on the sidewalk than let Preston think she was interested in being at the party with him.

"You texted you wanted to talk — which is never a good sign — and then you and I never talked." Discreetly, Pres lifted his elbow for her to take. Of course, she didn't right away, so he was forced to grind out the last thought. "Though you may not believe it, I know you enough to know when you might self-destruct. And, personally, I don't want to see you actually self-destruct."

Well, that's annoying.

"Bella, I know you don't want to be here." He slipped in close to her. New flashes and that weight that had lifted tried to settle again, this time on her stomach, but when she didn't back away, Pres continued, "*I* asked you because I wanted to spend time with you."

"That's almost believable. Are you sure you don't want something else?"

They'd been standing there long enough that the flashes died down. The crowds of photographers and a few journalists held a collective breath to see if Bella Astor did something newsworthy.

Preston stepped into her line of sight, making her look at him. "Bella Astor," he held his arm out for her again and said, "I would like to be your date tonight."

"Ugh! You think you're so suave."

"If Bella Astor has all but agreed to be my date, I think suave is the correct adjective."

She slipped her hand into the crook of his arm and let him lead her into the Astor brownstone. "I'm not your date."

"Close enough."

Stepping through the threshold, Bella was overcome. Like this house had thrown her back in time. Not that Daniel's speech, stuck in her mind, helped any. She relished a glimpse at the restored molding and woodwork Lina spent so much time perfecting with contractors. The house felt proper and complete, yet it held history. Bella saw some of her grandparents' furniture from the entryway, like the carved wood of a familiar couch in the sitting room. It transported her back to when she'd run through her grandparents' own brownstone with Chris in tow. They chased after Preston during their holiday parties until her father found them and started a new game.

"Act natural," Preston sang in her ear as he dropped his hands on her shoulders.

"Why?" Dumbest question ever. Bella had zero time to react. "Oh, shit. Mother."

"An impeccable greeting if I've ever heard one," Lina sighed.

"We are humbled to be invited at all, Mrs. Astor."

The charm was so thick that Bella thought she might suffocate.

"Speak for yourself."

"Excuse me, Bella dear, did you..."

"I'm sorry, mother. I'll speak louder. I said... speak. For. Yourself. You blackmailed me into being here." More weight lifted, and there was an ease slipping into Bella. She felt comfortable and oddly at home.

Preston squeezed her shoulders, telling her to stop.

"Preston!" Ah, the first of what was sure to be many interruptions by someone Preston needed to speak with. "I've been waiting for you."

"Bella... I need..." A frantic yet well-established panic came over Preston.

"To run off? You're not even my date and ditching me."

"I am your date." His glower deepened. "Five minutes."

"You say that about a lot of things." Bella gave Preston a sarcastic half-curtsey as he excused himself from her mother.

Lina wasted no time. "Well, you both are a vision together."

"Then you might need to visit the optometrist, mother. Everything must be blurry for you."

Using his impeccable timing, her brother parted the crowd, holding two champagne flutes aloft. Ever the dashing gentleman, Christian's curls were the opposite of hers. Wild and carefree.

Bella took the proffered flute and emptied it in several unseemly gulps.

"A warm welcome to my dear sister!" Chris teased.

"What? Are you stuck in a regency romance?"

"Bella," her mother droned.

"Speaking of warm," Bella replaced her empty flute and stole the second in her brother's hand. "I'm feeling warm." Plucking the ribbon on the wrap, Bella let it fall to the floor and was off to the party without any other comments to her mother.

"Dear sister," Chris sang when he caught up, dropping his empty flute with a passing server.

"What of it, dumbass?"

After appraising her for a moment, Chris grinned devilishly. "Love the dress."

Both twins burst into fits of boisterous laughter. Christian took his sister's arm. They toured around the party, snickering to one another, patently ignoring or skirting around families neither could stand.

Many people attempted to call on Christian. As CEO of Astor Pharm, he should have been mingling, networking, buttering up the governor over in the corner, the senator wooing the middle Beaton daughter, and so on. But he wasn't. Chris firmly planted himself with Bella, like when they were kids, teens, and even adults. He was by her side, and Preston was nowhere to be seen. A true throwback to five years ago.

It was only when Bella was alone for thirty seconds – Chris off to fetch round four on the champagne and Preston was *shockingly* not returned from his schmoozing – that the inevitable happened.

"How does trash even get into a gala as fine as this?"

CHAPTER TWENTY
Standing up

Lucas

He'd been parked in the small lot behind the recreational center for twenty minutes, rummaging up the courage to go inside but instead replayed what happened in Bella's apartment. Waiting for the right time, being Bella's friend, was all well and good, but listening to Lina, staying away from the party, felt like a betrayal of his friendship with her. Or his love for Bella.

Eli had always invited Lucas to every function or party or trip (even if Lucas couldn't attend), constantly commenting on the shift he'd seen in the twins with Lucas around. And while Eli may not have said it, Eli seemed to sense Lucas was Bella's moral support. Eli barely treated Lucas and Chris any differently; Lucas was part of the Astor family. Being banned from the gala was like an affront to Eli's memory.

But going into the rec center alone was equally wrong. This was Bella's night again. Her party, her work, her kids, and her families.

A text pinged. Probably Chris trying to admonish him or Alicia asking where he was. It could wait. He had enough self-loathing to take care of any admonishment they had in store for him.

Alicia: *I'm getting notifications of recent activity in hashtags most used for Bella. Dare I look?*

Since he'd yet to work up the nerve to go into the rec center party, and even if Alicia didn't dare look, Lucas opened his browser and searched for Bella's name. There were several pictures of B on her mother's brownstone sidewalk, mid-verbal assault on Preston. Nothing too incriminating.

But there was one picture that stood out; not quite trending yet, probably because it was the newest picture. Bella, without her wrap, walked through the ballroom. People gaped openly at her, pointed, whispered behind hands, and it was obvious what they were talking about. But her stride, her posture never faltered. Bella was the epitome of grace and confidence, right down to the gleam in her eyes.

This confidence, though, would be easily broken. Lucas had never even noticed, but the most prominent part of the picture was a portion of the scar from her collarbone surgery. The scar was always there; he saw it plenty but never thought twice about it. The scar was part of her, this tangible reminder of the good she brought to the small corners of the world she'd traveled to.

Lucas hit Chris' name on his call log, knuckles turned white, gripping the steering wheel while he waited for his friend to pick up.

Chris answered with an annoyed whisper, "I'm trying to keep Bella from murdering our mother's guests."

For the gala, it was still early. Murmurs behind Chris, not music and dancing. All the mingling Bella hated most.

"I'm coming."

"That's... interesting. Mother banned you from the premises."

They both waited as Lucas started his car again.

When he finally relented,

Chris said, "I'll meet you in the back."

Bella

Lory Beaumont. There wasn't even a point to turning around. The sneer, the haughtiness, and dripping disdain hadn't changed in the last decade.

Bella also didn't need to turn around to find Cissy Blase and Jemma Muir, Lory's clique in high school, surrounding her. But she did, and there was very little to be surprised about.

Every school had *those* girls, from public to the poshest private schools. And in adulthood, *those* girls turned into *those* women, at least where these three were concerned. Lory Beaumont was just as insufferable, egotistical, and starved for attention and drama as ever. Therefore, she needed to create her own.

Normally, Bella would not engage. A nagging voice, annoyingly Preston's, but inside her head, said, *"Be an adult. Be civil."*

Except this was Bella's house. If she was going to stand up for herself, this (or any Astor estate) is the first place.

Bella's turn was slow and deliberate. A serene smile tugged at her lips. She refused to cower. Instead, she kept herself tall with perfect posture.

Lory used to switch between hair colors to whatever was most popular. Currently, she sported platinum blond hair, toned to the same perfection as her body. She was the type of woman who belonged at these events. Her elegant red gown adorned with intricate leaves, berries, and flowers embroidered into the outer layer of taffeta was bold like her.

But the Beaumonts weren't the Astors in title or status. They aspired to be the next Astors, but that road was long and unlikely to occur in Lory's generation.

"I see you're reduced to wearing designers off the racks now, hmm?" Bella said, not trying to but kind of copying Lory's tone.

Lory faltered.

With caramel-colored hair and a gown of deep navy blue with queen-style sleeves, Jemma clearly avoided Bella's eyes. Cissy, who'd always felt like a clone of Lory's, and had platinum blond hair, stepped away from her friend.

"Nice Robe, Cis. Very chic." Bella gave the woman a wry grin, nodding at the dress, and Cissy smoothed a wrinkle away. "Very much from a year ago, huh?"

There was a lot people did not expect of Bella. One was that she studiously did her homework, even when she didn't want to. Fashion, for example, was a thing she *never* wanted to study but did for just these moments.

"Well," Lory recovered and said, "We understand our place. And we're not broken dolls content to sit on a shelf and repeat our mistakes."

"Lory's oldest *is* on track for early admission to..." Jemma's confidence needled under Bella's skin, causing Bella's glare to turn to 11, and Jemma stuttered, "N-nightingale?"

The woman was trying to diffuse Lory's animosity and maybe even Bella's. Still, it wouldn't sway either woman, and Lory only shushed her friend.

Bella's chest heaved, and her hands shook. "I'm not sure what you mean by broken, *Lory*."

"You..."

Soft hands slid across Bella's back, sending a wave of goosebumps flying up. "Bella!" Preston's grin gleamed at each woman, landing last on Bella before falling away completely. He even paled as he stared, rather openly, at her chest.

"I'd suggest a plastic surgeon, but I doubt there's anything they could do to fix *that*." Lory gestured to all of Bella.

Stepping out of Preston's grip, Bella settled her breath and said, "That's fine. I'd never use someone that did... *that* to you."

The stunned silence radiated to the guests nearby. And, of all people, Preston's composure completely evaporated. The man didn't even bother to feign a smile at Bella.

As Preston latched onto her arm, Lory and her clique melted away into the guests and whispered, "You had to make a scene?"

"Excuse me?" Bella shoved him off of her. "Make a scene?"

Oh, *now* she'd make a scene?

"Let's go somewhere private."

"Let's not," Bella said, standing her ground.

"You wore a dress like *that* on purpose, Bella. What did you expect?"

"I expected people to act like adults. It's a scar. It's not some obscene gesture..."

"It's ridiculous. I... I need some air."

The guests parted for Preston, soft murmurs following him and Bella as she chased him down.

"This is ridiculous?"

Preston shook his head, refusing to speak as he kept walking through the side door, the kitchen, and the back garden.

The back patio was relatively spacious. Three brownstones worth of yards opened up to make one patio and a flower garden. A prominent New England arbor reached across a third of the patio, intertwined with vines and decorated with twinkling lights, which, under normal circumstances, would be romantic. The arbor extended to the patio's edge before a path wound through the grass around the flower garden and a few cherry blossom trees until exiting at the garage and back alley.

"What's ridiculous," Bella's tone grew harsher the longer Pres tried to storm away from her, "is that you can't even look at me! I'm your date, for crying out loud!"

"Now you're my date? Because until now, you could barely stand to be around me."

Her stomach roiled! How often had he been her date and not been there for her? Bella argued back, seething, "Maybe I'd be more excited about the prospect if you stood up for me! Just once!"

Their voices echoed among the houses, rising over the party's noise.

Two huge strides and Preston was in her face saying, "I stick up for you all the time, but you — *you* — make it so hard to keep fighting for you when you act so insanely childish!"

"What is childish about accepting, hell, loving myself? This dress is fabulous and..."

"And you wore it just for the shock value, Bella! You're not 18 anymore!"

"No! I'm an adult. Who was injured helping people, Preston! Who saved lives!"

"You could have covered it up! Had it fixed! Not make yourself purposely stand out! That part of your life is finally over. And I waited for you because I love you. And now we can move on!"

"Move on?" Bella broke away. "Move on from what?"

"You did the whole 'save people' bullshit. Now you can put it behind you, and we can..."

"Put it behind me? What makes you think I want to 'put it behind me?'"

In his agitation, Preston circled her, undoing the buttons on his jacket, even loosening his tie before he said, "You're not entertaining going back?" Then he let out a slightly deranged sort of laugh.

Bella blinked. She hadn't really thought that through. Sure, she'd been injured, but Bella hadn't ruled out returning to Frontier Doctors. Maybe some of her family thought she wouldn't, but... her father kept returning. She wanted to be just like him.

"Bella, that's..."

"And what if I go back?" she recoiled again from Pres as he held his hand for hers.

Preston turned towards the roses, or where they should be, come summer.

"Can you not even look at me? Is the scar that disgusting to you?"

She moved into his line of sight, and Preston flinched. Bending at the waist, Bella caught a few breaths, and when she stood again, she couldn't bring herself up to her full height.

"Why can Lucas tell me I look beautiful, and you can barely stand the sight of me?"

Pres made a popping sound with his lips. "I wonder." After heaving a great sigh, Preston locked eyes with her. The eyes that sent swaths of women into hysterics, burned with passion, and smoldered were now filled with ire. "Your father only did those 'Frontier Doctor trips' as a PR stunt. He never..."

It wasn't the tears stinging her eyes again or the way her blood boiled that stopped Bella's heart. It was Chris careening out the doorway, crushing Preston's jaw with a weak, floppy-fisted punch, then immediately regretting the action.

"Leave filthy lies about our father out of your mouth! Holy crap, that hurt!" Chris was reduced to one knee and tears. "How do you do that all the time?"

Bella wasn't sure she had words for what had just happened.

But a singular set of applause came from behind her.

Lucas stood behind her, beaming, his applause getting louder and faster as if a crowd would follow.

Bella said, "You punch with a closed fist, you dumbass." She gave her brother's shoulder a squeeze. A new round of heat rose in Bella's chest at seeing Lucas.

Rubbing his jaw, Preston made to say something when Chris interrupted, "Ugh! If you can't stand up for Bella, you don't deserve to be with her."

The brownstone stood over them. The joyous string quartet Bella's mother hired began their first set. There'd be dancing, excessive drinking, and more gossip than Bella could stomach.

Bella walked towards Lucas on shaking feet, throwing a "Goodbye, Preston" over her shoulder.

Lucas patiently waited, his applause over, hands stuffed in his pockets, for her to reach him. All of Bella's energy drained from her. Walking, even standing upright, was a chore on unsteady legs.

Lucas didn't ask if she was okay or upset when she arrived. He asked, "Are you cold?"

"No?" Of course, Bella's voice betrayed her, but Lucas continued to stand there, beaming at her.

"You still look beautiful."

The Astor brownstone, the party, the eyes, the whispers, Bella turned her back on all of it. Part of her wanted to return, but a more significant part couldn't do it again. At least not tonight.

"I need to... leave or something. And you can't come in... according to my mother. But there's another party..."

"Good, because Alicia might kill me. I never made it into the rec center. She's been there by herself all night."

A suit jacket landed across her shoulders, bringing blessed warmth. Chris expertly snaked one arm around her and continued to shake out the glorious hand he'd stupidly open-fisted punched with. "I need to have some extra words with our lawyer."

"Do we need to call another lawyer? You going to take more pages from Bella's book?" The joke lit up Lucas' face even more, and Bella tried to take a mental snapshot so she'd never forget.

"No. Her book is very painful."

"Closed fist. Like literally the simplest rule."

Her brother yanked her into him and pecked her cheek. Had he ever done that before?

"See you at the other party, B." Chris gave her another squeeze and disappeared into their family home, searching for Preston.

CHAPTER TWENTY-ONE
What's this?

Lucas

Bella shivered the entire way to his car, which was parked at the head of the alley, but she refused to say one word about it. He continued shuffling to keep Chris' suit jacket closed around Bella until they were in the car, and she blasted the heat.

Perfect timing for Lucas' car to decide the heat didn't need to work.

It didn't matter. Bella was away from the party and Preston. She seemed to melt into the seat, utterly silent other than her chattering teeth, until, "No, I don't want to talk. Just drive."

"You got it." Lucas made the dumb mistake of glancing at Bella. One glance and his brilliant mind was left numb.

"What?" she snapped.

He should have looked away sooner. He knew precisely how Bella captured his attention. Why he didn't know better by now was beyond him. "Nothing. I'm just proud of you."

Many emotions crossed her face, some melting together and unreadable. She grunted, and Lucas took the hint and started driving as the first tears rolled down her cheeks.

She hated — or loathed with every fiber of her being — anyone seeing her cry or be weak.

Weaving through the streets, Lucas hit traffic only a few blocks away from the Astor brownstone, and they were moving at a snail's pace. Bella heaved a few deep sighs. His hand slid across the center console, palm up, and her freezing hand slapped into his.

They were thoroughly stuck in bumper-to-bumper traffic and going nowhere fast. Some local station played Christmas music so low Lucas could only hear a faint melody when his car idled.

Bella wiped her face with her free hand while squeezing his hand even tighter.

This. Now. Just say it.

"Bella...?"

Her yelp scared the crap out of him. Both let go and jumped, though from what Lucas wasn't sure until Bella produced her cell phone from a hidden pocket among the many, many, many folds of cloth that made up her gown.

"Chris?" Bella's puckered, sour face paired perfectly with an eye roll. "Bet he needs a ride and regrets not leaving with us?"

When Bella answered, she put the call on speaker and moved in with an immediate kill shot for her twin. "We're not turning around, you dumbass! Just get a driver..."

"Are you Bella Astor?" A woman, rather professional if exhausted sounding, asked.

Lucas tried to place the voice but couldn't.

"Yes," Bella drew the word out, as confused as Lucas. "And you are?"

"Your brother asked me to call you. I'm an EMT. We're heading to Mt. Sinai, but he requested I call you now."

"EMT? What the fuck happened?"

"Mr. Astor?" The woman sounded like she was sitting next to Chris, and he was moaning. In pain. Not... not the other way. "Mr. Astor?" she repeated softly.

"Ugh! I got into a car accident. Are you happy?"

The call dropped, leaving Lucas trying to figure out how to turn out of this traffic and get them to Mt. Sinai.

Bella

"I'll murder him!" Bella tore through the emergency room. Pushing past nurses and doctors.

Patients, which overflowed from the rooms into the hallways, gaped at her gown, and a few brave nurses recognized Bella and stopped her to say hi. But she would not be deterred.

"Where is he?" She stopped at the nurses' station and glared.

"Evening, Dr. B.," a kind nurse named Walter, his big blocky glasses who always made an impression on Bella, pointed across the hall. Walter was as disheveled as he usually was, his short black hair mostly hidden under a scarf tied over it. "Your brother is there. We're waiting on the results from radiology."

"You'll have to send him back to radiology when I'm done with him."

Lucas caught up and opened his mouth to say something, but Bella stormed right off again into the room Walter indicated.

"Good luck, Mr. Astor," Walter smirked and returned to his charting work.

"Bella?" Lucas said as he tried to catch up with her again.

But she burst through a curtained wall of a temporary room and howled, "You were driving?"

"Oh, delightful. You're here," Bella's brother drawled, pressing himself further into his flat hospital pillow.

Yes, she was there. It only took an hour in New York's forsaken traffic!

They wrapped one of Chris' wrists in a stiff brace. His fingers were swollen and tight.

"You broke your wrist?" She sat on the bed's edge, pressing into her brother to check his eyes and a forming bruise on his cheek. And leaned in further to hiss, "Why the fuck were you driving?"

His eyes flicked behind her, and Bella noticed a nurse standing there, mouth hanging open now, actively trying to look away. And she was blushing.

"Ah. I get it. You were flirting with the nurses, too? First of all..." Each word was a struggle to keep her rage contained and muscular arms wrapped around her, keeping Bella from attacking her idiot brother.

The nurse scurried through the curtain wall, and Lucas kept hold for dear life.

"What the hell were you thinking?"

"I was pissed off, Bella! I always thought Pres, my friend, would treat my sister better! And then he said..."

"So, what? *You* left for a leisurely drive?" Bella kicked to get free, but Lucas was strong and held her well.

"I... I..."

The curtain parted, and an ER doctor walked in, gaping at Bella. "D-Dr. B?"

Still struggling against Lucas, Bella said, "Hello, *Dr. Pearson.*"

A man, about Bella's age, with dull dark blond hair and pale skin, gave the scene a once over and kept reading his notes.

"I should have known. Mr. Astor has a broken wrist and..."

"And we're going to add to that," Bella growled.

"Bella, big breaths!" Lucas said, still fighting to keep her from pouncing.

"Whoever you are, sir, we thank you for your service." Dr. Pearson's face lifted a bit, adding, "Looks like Mr. Astor does not have a concussion, which is fortunate. Could have avoided that altogether if Dr. B wasn't called."

Chris sighed and ran his uninjured hand through his messy curls. "She's my emergency contact."

"That's unfortunate for you." Dr. Pearson kept an utter deadpan the entire time. "We'll finish up the paperwork. Discharge you."

"You can keep me here. I will sit in a corner..."

Pearson had the dead stare of a doctor on hour 14 of a 12-hour shift. "We're discharging you, Mr. Astor. It's a broken wrist. I'd say you shouldn't drink and drive next time, but your BAC was zero."

"Wait. Zero? You were drinking with me for like an hour before Preston and I..." Bella took stock of her own body. She wasn't drunk either, even after four champagnes.

"Mother switched to sparkling grape juice and other non-alcoholic drinks for most at the Christmas gala after a disaster last year and..."

That garnered a renewed howl from Bella.

"Get well soon, Mr. Astor." A cold flash crossed Pearson's eyes.

"Keep me here!" Chris called again.

In the same deadpan, Pearson said, "Hell no. You're Dr. B's brother. I'm not that stupid, and you've got tall, handsome, and blond there. Maybe you won't be back tonight."

Lucas's grip on Bella had loosened, but now he tightened again.

"A car? You hadn't driven since your driver's test when we were 16!"

"That is wildly inaccurate," Chris said, resigned to the torment he was about to endure. "I drove that one time after getting my license. By the way, your stranglehold on Manhattan medical treatment is awe-inspiring."

Lucas

Chris wrecked a Porsche. What model? Who knows? Lucas didn't pay much attention to that kind of stuff, and the pictures on Chris' phone were of a twisted pile of metal and tires that did not currently resemble a car. He also tried to keep his attention on driving back to their condos and preventing Bella from launching herself into the backseat to murder her twin.

The struggle continued from Lucas' car to the elevator and all the way into Chris' condo.

"No, really! Explain it to me! What possessed you today, of *all days,* to get behind the wheel of a car?"

"I told you!" Chris threw himself through his door, trying to get away.

Lucas grappled with Bella, but he could only keep his grip on her arms or torso for a moment before she wiggled free. Chris was frantic to get to safety and tried shutting the door on her, but Bella slammed into it before Chris could close the door. And she was advancing again.

"Bella. We might all need to take a step back... breathe."

"I'm breathing just fine!" She was fighting with all her remaining strength. Thankfully for Chris, she wasn't as fast as usual. "Mother seemed rather nonplussed about her *dumbass* son stealing a car..."

"I own the car," Chris said on his way around the breakfast bar.

"It's a family vehicle, you twat!"

"I bought it for mother! My name is on the title!"

All Chris' stupidity brought was renewed growls from Bella and her chasing him through his condo straight into his bedroom. Where he locked the door, leaving Bella to smash her palm against the wood.

"Well," Lucas said, standing at the door of the condo because what else was there to do when two siblings in their 30s were chasing each other like they were six? "Don't inflict bodily harm while I..."

A string of profanities from Bella changed Lucas' mind. He wanted to get her something to wear, not her ball gown, and maybe a blanket. But leaving Bella alone in the condo with her brother was not an appropriate option. She might remember how to pick a lock and actually get into her brother's bedroom, and then they really would be back at the ER.

Next to the door was a bag of dirty laundry sitting out for Chris' cleaning service to clean. The plastic tore easily, and Lucas rifled for a pair of lounge pants and t-shirt and threw them clear across the room, hitting Bella in the back.

"I'm not leaving," she insisted and slammed on the bedroom door again.

"Didn't think you would, Bells. Get changed." Lucas tossed the winter jacket off and fell next to it. "I'm not leaving you alone with Chris."

"You're the wisest of us all!" Chris shouted from the door.

"No!" Lucas shouted back. "That would be Alicia for not being with us tonight."

Lucky woman.

Bella emerged from Chris' bathroom a few minutes later, leaving behind a sparkling pile of satin on the bathroom floor and her brother's suit jacket. When Lucas peeked in, the jacket was in a soaking heap on the floor. She gave her brother's bedroom door a passing slap, and the door rattled in response as if Chris were sitting against it and jumped.

"Come out here, and I'll show you how I really feel," Bella seethed.

"Holt! Convince my sister to get the fuck out of my house!"

Lucas responded with a quick, "No." He hadn't needed to know them for years to learn not to get in the middle of their arguments. Even if the fight was mostly incoherent screaming and Bella threatening bodily harm to her brother.

Bella rested on the couch's armrest, staring daggers at the door. Whenever there was a sound, she threw a pillow at the door, and there were renewed scramblings. Eventually, she ran out of pillows and had to pick them up again.

Lucas turned on a movie, the volume reasonably low, so Bella could hear what her brother was up to and pounce when the time was right. Honestly, for as worried as they'd been when the EMT called, Lucas was grateful for a distraction for Bella. Bella had spent so much time worrying about Preston that this was a reprieve.

Bella tucked her feet under Lucas' legs to keep warm. Rightly refusing to wear Chris' dirty socks. When a shiver passed through her, Lucas draped his jacket over her like a blanket. A few minutes later, Bella drifted off and fell against Lucas' chest.

But he would not let Chris know. Let the jerk stew in his room all night.

Bella

A commercial invaded Bella's dream, snapping her out of a world where she was in a stadium, wrestling her brother in professional wrestling style. Costumes. Chairs. Cage matches. Bella was winning, and now she was back in her brother's bare, overtly ugly contemporary condo.

Lucas' aftershave, a rosemary and musk scent that reeked of Chris (as in a gift), greeted her. He'd untied his tie, and fallen asleep in his contacts again, which meant his eyes would be bugging him all day. The clock read just past 5 am on Christmas Eve. Lucas was leaving today for his family celebration.

Bella turned down the TV and wrapped herself tighter in the jacket but stopped before resting her head against Lucas again.

Confusion and doubt swirled from her stomach to her head. Part of her said stay, rest where she'd been resting. Where she always slept best. With Lucas on the couch, snuggling.

Part of her screamed to leave. Give him space, and live his life. Like she'd been trying to do!

A red paper slipped from the jacket's pocket, crinkling loudly when Bella shifted. She grabbed it to toss on the table until she noticed her name written on the front. A ribbon tied in a handsome bow kept the letter together. Bella pulled the ribbon and unfolded the paper as quietly as she could.

Inside was a letter, written in Lucas' doctor-like penmanship.

Bella,

For how many times I've written this letter, both in my mind and in reality, this is the best I've been able to do. But you deserve so much more.

Since the moment we met, there hasn't been a time when you weren't the one picking me up. Whether I was at my lowest or not. You were there. When we met, you couldn't have known how close to quitting Columbia I was. My life has changed for the better every day since meeting you.

I've struggled to tell you how much you mean to me, Bella. And no time will ever feel like the right time, but I needed you to know that I love you.

Merry Christmas

Lucas

Bella's vision went blurry. Hot, fat tears falling dropped onto Chris' white tee. She had to reread the letter a few times, and even then, Bella felt shaky and unsteady.

How had she not known? Did she know?

She'd always wanted to be around Lucas back in college. Maybe part of her even wanted more until her grandfather shot down any dreams of being with *anyone* he disapproved of.

And her grandfather *certainly* disapproved of Lucas after one time when Preston tricked Lucas into joining an Astor party without an invitation. It had been the catalyst for sending Bella to a finishing school.

Lucas was her constant. She always loved him, but she never thought about what kind of love she had for him.

She loved Lucas.

Bella couldn't imagine her life without Lucas in it.

Beside her, Lucas shifted, sitting up a little straighter and murmuring her name in his half-asleep state.

Crushing the edge of the letter in her hand, Bella threw herself into Lucas, her arms around his neck. Lucas woke with a start, and before he could say anything, Bella kissed him.

Lucas

The world was still a fog, like before actually waking up. A sudden warmth and weight confused Lucas, but it was probably just Bella...

A crushing squeeze grabbed his neck, quickly giving way to a soft yet urgent press of lips against his. Long hair fell against his cheeks and hands as he brushed her cheek.

Her. Cheek?

The only 'her' he was with was Bella. So the only 'her' that could be kissing him was Bella.

A shuddering gasp and Bella pulled away, only the barest amount before Lucas closed the gap again, no thoughts other than giving in.

This time the kiss deepened, Bella climbing onto his lap. He'd felt her sleep against him for years, but this was different. It was...

Slam!

A pillow smacked both Bella and Lucas' faces bringing them to an abrupt stop. Bella pulled away, and she sported a familiar scowl.

"*Finally!* You two took way too long." Then Chris yelped and careened into the kitchen when Bella hopped over the couch back after him.

"Too long? Says the asshole who drove when he doesn't *drive!*" The kitchen island stood between the two siblings. Bella feinted one way then the other, trying hard to lure Chris to her.

This wasn't a dream.

Holy shit, it wasn't a dream.

Lucas wanted to throw up. How... what... just *how* did this happen?

A paper resting on the back of the couch scratched his neck. The letter had been in his jacket.

Short, sharp gasps gripped Lucas. Bella read his letter.

Bella read... the words...

He pressed into his chest, willing his body to work right.

"Better help the guy out. Lucas might pass out!" Chris tried to divert her attention, but Bella wouldn't be swayed. She dove for her brother and chased him into the living room again as he raced into the safety of his bedroom once more.

Lucas stood, his knees threatening to give out, and caught Bella loosely in the living room, already feeling dizzy. "Bella, I can explain."

She wheeled around to face him, and suddenly they were way too close together. "Why didn't you ever say anything?" The crazed look was mainly gone.

Lucas dropped Bella, staggering back. "I-I... Bella... how could I screw up the best thing..."

He wasn't sure what to expect when she launched herself at him again. But he was pleasantly surprised that it ended with Bella jumping on him (not actually unusual, she did that often) and a kiss. Tender and short, leaving Lucas' brain fog even worse than when he first woke.

"You should have said something sooner." Her eyes closed, and she leaned her forehead against his. Lucas closed his eyes and felt her breath on his cheek.

She'd read the words he'd always wanted to say, but trying to say them out loud took every ounce of courage. "I-I love you, Bella."

Christian

Who knew when it would be safe to come out of his room again. Chris slid down against his locked door and then played with the velcro on the wrist brace. All he'd wanted was a yogurt and to use the bathroom. At least the physical torture of Bella and Lucas was over.

Still sitting on the charger next to his bed, his phone rang with a haunting melody.

Mother's ringtone.

"Good morning, mother!"

"Please tell me it's all over, finally?"

"Bella and Lucas?" Chris sighed. "Oh, my word. Was that all you?"

"Not all of it," Lina said, her tone as biting as ever. "But it was bordering on the absurd."

"I want no other details, mother. Or Bella will be taking over responsibilities as CEO because I will be rotting in a gutter somewhere."

"Give your sister some credit. She's brilliant enough to dispose of you properly."

"Mother! Was that a compliment?" Chris asked, but the call had already ended.

CHAPTER TWENTY-TWO
Epilogue

Lucas

Chris stared, uncomfortably intent on both Bella and Lucas on the drive to Bella's apartment so she could rush and put a bag together. Then to Laguardia, into the Astor jet, and the entire freaking flight to Kalamazoo.

On the plane, Bella threw pillows and shoes, and Lucas had to catch her before she chucked the crystal bowl filled with Christian's favorite mints.

"Well, do something already!" Chris whined, and with a depressingly weak toss, a pillow landed at their feet.

Lucas squeezed his eyes shut tight because his question was surely a mistake, but he still asked, "Do what?"

"Act all lovey-dovey! You're not kissing, or making out, or anything!"

Out of spite, Bella moved across the bench seat and pulled out a book from her purse, keeping her middle finger up as she read.

Lucas flushed. When Chris dared to emerge from his room again earlier in the morning, Bella and Lucas may have been very engrossed in certain... activities on his couch. Chris snapped for them to get a room, so Lucas picked Bella up and carried her to his apartment to give Chris a reprieve.

That had been enough of a pause for Lucas' senses to kick in. He'd felt intense guilt when he asked Bells to stop kissing him and then pulled away.

"I... don't want to... uh," Lucas felt very at home, returning to a loss of words around Bella. They were lying in his bed. How could he have brought her straight there?

"Don't want to what?" Bella asked.

"I don't want to rush things," he'd blurted out. "We've been friends for such a long time, and for as well as I know you, I don't know what you'd want in a relationship."

Bella grabbed his neck, flipped Lucas onto his back, and pecked him on the cheek once, twice, and then on his lips. "Ok."

"Ok?"

"Ok."

They'd spent the morning talking, stealing kisses, and figuring out how they would move forward. No switch instantly flipped, and they'd be in a perfect relationship. Bella was too important of a person for him to rush into a romance with.

In the jet, Chris was still staring at them. "What happened? How did you screw it up?"

"He did nothing!" Bella called.

There was a definite slump in Chris' posture, and he played with the edges of his brace. "You didn't sleep with her?"

"Why are you even asking that?" Lucas asked, his cheeks on fire. "She's your sister!"

"Of course." He was shaking his head at them both. "But twelve years warrant some extreme measures. What are you doing to show Bella you love her and not screw it up?"

Lucas leaned across the gap a little further and grumbled, "I will not screw it up!"

After landing, the annoying glances, sneers, and commentary continued on the drive to Lucas' parents' house.

For a late December mid-afternoon in Michigan, the sky was overcast as far as the eye could see. Not the clouds that threatened snow. The kind that made everything feel gloomy. Unlike in New York, there was over two feet of snow, and on street corners and parking lots, the piles were taller than Lucas. Though still fresh enough, the banks were primarily white and not a murky gray color.

The front of his parents' split-level house was decorated with colorful lights lining all the gutters and windows, plastic light-up reindeer, and Santa Claus figures as old as Lucas.

His mom and dad were lounging in the kitchen when Lucas stomped his boots on the welcome mat. Lexi, her bright blond hair thrown up in a messy bun, popped up from behind her phone on the couch to slap Lucas with a pillow on his way in.

Bella blocked, ripped the pillow free, and bopped Christian in the face.

"Bella?" Lexi perked up, tossing herself over the couch, straight into Bella, shrieking incoherently. His younger sister didn't abide by rules, very much like Bella. Though in her mid-20s, she didn't let her enthusiasm diminish. "Bella! Oh, it's been so long!"

They stood there, Lexi wrapped around Bella's torso, reminiscent of the first Christmas Lucas brought Bella and Chris home with him.

Bella's eyes were glassy, but she held her composure until Lucas' mom came rushing out with a slew of, "Oh, dear! You're home!"

"She's been home, mom," Lucas whispered.

"Of course, but not here, at home." His mom enveloped Bella, too, turning her cheeks a bright pink.

It took a while for the Holt household to calm down.

Bella set her bag in Lexi's old bedroom, a room that had practically become a time capsule of Lexi's life. Her old unicorn duvet, piles of stuffed animals that did not make the move to his sister's apartment, along with her banged-up dresser and bedside tables.

The men stood at the door of Lucas' childhood room and single twin bed.

"Bunk with Bella," Chris whined.

"No."

Lucas would take the basement couch like he did many years Bella joined them.

"Twelve years, and you're doing everything in your power to lose my sister." Chris' whiny complaint was loud enough for Bella to hear and retaliate by whipping a pillow through the connecting bathroom. She successfully hit Chris to Lexi's cheers echoing through their old bedrooms. Bella closed off the bathroom, and she didn't emerge again for nearly an hour.

"I don't need to sleep with Bella to keep her."

Her brother had worked his brotherly magic getting under her skin. Chris and Lucas joined his parents in the kitchen. Fresh, strong eggnog and cookies were out, and cookbooks surrounded Lexi searching for a new cookie recipe.

"How many varieties did you and B agree to?"

"B? Aren't you freaking cool?" Lexi flicked her brother's hand off her head. "And three kinds. But I still haven't nailed down the third. Bella pulled out the licitars recipe. We forgot some stuff and need to run up to the store."

Movement in the living room near the tree caught Lucas' eyes. Bella had finally emerged, hugging her arms tight, and studied the Holt Christmas tree.

Christmas Eve.

"Hey, big, fancy New York businessman! You coming with dad and me?" Lex asked.

"Ah, no. You can handle it without me, right?" He grabbed two glasses and ladled some eggnog into each, adding a sprinkle of nutmeg exactly as his mom had taught him.

Lex said, "Sure?" Gazing at Lucas on his way past, his sister opened her mouth to say something else but never got the words out.

Walking up behind Bella, he let out a small huff, brought her glass over her head, and held it at eye level. Since he was standing at her shoulder, he caught the turn of her mouth upward.

"Our first Christmas here." Bella took the mug and pointed at a pink and purple painted popsicle stick frame containing a picture of Bella, Lucas, and Chris on the brown sectional couch in the basement.

He had never noticed how Bella leaned into him before in those pictures. Her head rested on his shoulder even back in her first year of college.

Abruptly, Bella turned to face him. She'd never put on makeup today, not that it mattered. Bella was more radiant like this. Dewy skin and flushed cheeks.

"I thought you were going to do something cheesy." After everything with Preston in the last day and the gala, and Chris' accident, Lucas promised her space, and Chris had pushed the last button his sister had left. Finally, Bella seemed to be coming back around. Her smile was warm, and his heart raced again.

"Cheesy?" Lucas touched an old silk mistletoe his mom hung in the hallway every year in his back pocket. He made his move, and when she glanced down at the eggnog in her hand, he held it over them. "Why would I do something cheesy?"

A silent giggle from Bella brought a smile to his face. She glanced up, and there it was.

"I love when you're cheesy." Raising up on her tiptoes, Bella looped her arms around his neck, careful not to spill the eggnog. Their lips brushed together, leaving a tingling behind every time they parted.

A glass shattered, and an excited screech startled them apart.

"What! *What?* You two? *Dad!* Lucas and Bella! This is not a drill!"

Curls peeked out from around the kitchen door. "Huh," Chris said, "I guess you didn't screw up."

Lucas dropped the mistletoe, but Bella kept nuzzling his cheek with her nose.

"Was *everyone* waiting for you to say something?" she asked.

"Yeah," he answered. "Wait, you and Lex were in her room forever. You didn't tell her?"

"No. She's your sister. I dealt with Chris."

Immature giggles preceded Chris yelling, "Get a room!"

"You didn't deal with him enough," Lucas sighed.

She whispered, "I dumped snow in his boots and shoes." Then to her brother, "Chris, go shopping with Lex!"

"Only if you'll..."

"Go!" Lucas and Bella said simultaneously.

Rocking them back and forth, Lucas kissed her temple and said, "He will kill us."

"I can take him."

Gazing into her eyes, Lucas noted the change. He brushed the hair back to get a better view of her eyes.

"What's on your mind, Bella Astor?"

"That I am pretty stupid for not seeing you before."

Lucas turned her back to the tree, the pictures of him and her dotting the branches encased in colorful popsicle stick frames over the years.

Bella leaned into him. Her weight and warmth stole his breath.

After a cough to clear his throat, Lucas pointed. "The way you looked at me just now?" She nodded. "I guess I missed it too all those years."

"I can't believe you let me push you to date someone! What is wrong with you?"

"I didn't tell you."

"Dumbass."

"You never needed a man to make you happy, though."

"I know." She sipped the eggnog thoughtfully. "I just needed to be around the people that I love."

Behind them, Lucas' parents and Lex ran commentary on them, snuggling into each other. Bella was a master at ignoring them, and Lucas concentrated on doing the same. "So, we didn't waste our time together."

"Nope."

About the Author

Mom of 3 who loves sci-fi, fantasy, anime, and k- & c-dramas. When not wrangling children she can be found hiding in a corner with a mug of tea and her laptop. Typing furiously and laughing at her own jokes.

Avid nerd, she hosts a blog called Nerdy Mom Writes, which updates when she feels the muse or is enthralled by some new nerdy exploit. When not writing her own original stories, she can also be found lurking around fanfiction, both writing and reading.

Read more at https://nerdymomwrites.com.

CPSIA information can be obtained
at www.ICGtesting.com
Printed in the USA
BVHW041735201022
649892BV00004B/359

9 798986 998206